TOUCH NO ONE

JOSEPH HIRSCH

BLACK  ROSE
writing™

The final approval for this literary material is granted by the author.

First printing

This is a work of fiction. Names, characters, businesses, places, events and incidents
are either the products of the author's imagination or used in a fictitious manner.
Any resemblance to actual persons, living or dead, or actual events is purely
coincidental.

ISBN: 978-1-61296-827-8
PUBLISHED BY BLACK ROSE WRITING
www.blackrosewriting.com

Printed in the United States of America
Suggested retail price $17.95

Touch No One is printed in Adobe Caslon Pro

For Tom Kakonis and David Atkinson

I've never read anything quite like it. John Moglich, an ex-cop turned house dick at the casino 'section' of Schengen City, a sprawling far-future metropolis balkanized into ethnic / sociopolitical divisions, hunts a genius-level, killer cyber-terrorist harvesting opiates (and something far more sinister) from mothers' milk...direct from the source, so to speak... This brief synopsis barely scratches the surface of how singularly strange this book is. Truth is, I barely know how to begin to summarize it. *Touch No One* is a work of extraordinary imagination, and high intelligence (high in both senses of the word). Hirsch has created a fully realized future world of Blade Runner neons, Avatar-like bio-luminescent vegetation, and Cronenbergian body modifications / 'enhancements.' It's a far future and yet feels disconcertingly contemporary in the characters' reliance on / addiction to technology diminishing human connection and physical contact. As bizarre as the premise might sound – and it is bizarre, often nightmarishly so – *Touch No One* is a surprisingly accessible read, tech-noir written in clean 'detective fiction' prose, veined with dry humor. I'll be interested to see what regular readers of sci-fi and cyberpunk make of it, so mark it down on your TBR list. For me, it was a mind-blowing read."

- Adam Howe, author of *Die Dog, or Eat the Hatchet*

TOUCH NO ONE

"The soul is an alien thing upon Earth."
~ Georg Trakl

CHAPTER ONE

THE RICHEST MAN IN THE CITY

I had spent the last three years as a house detective at the Zhakpot Hotel. I'd been making a comfortable living investigating dark coin thefts and credit swipes of various kinds, and I had no desire to return to the Schengen Force. Life was sometimes lonely in the kitsch palace, but this was the price I was willing to pay to be free from the dangers of police work and the complications of marriage.

"Sir…"

I had been staring out the wall-length window of my hotel room at the mock Vesuvius in the shadow of a very skeletal three-to-one scale replica of the Eifel Tower, when my service bot sent a subvoc message to my mastoid.

"What?" I turned from my view of the constantly erupting volcano, to the bot behind me. I had spoken out loud even though he had subvoc'd.

"Sir, there is an incoming message for you from a Bernard Blankstone."

My ears pricked up at the name and I stood. I didn't need to consult any of my mods to be impressed, and a little frightened. The richest man in Schengen had just contacted me.

"What does he want?" I moved over to my closet and selected a bespoke clamshell and slid it over my shoulders. I stood before my wall-length window, which looked out onto the Casino Node. The town was a kitschy nightmare collision of columns, arches, and pilasters that would have called to mind great ancient empires if it all wasn't offset by neon and undermined by tacky pirate ships, mermaids, and scaled version wonders of the world. The moon was rising above the Statue of Liberty in the distance as she bore her eternal light for the hopeless gamblers below.

"Mr. Blankstone requests your help with a matter he doesn't trust even to subvoc encryption." I straightened my clamshell jacket and stood face to face with my bot. Denholm was probably the classiest thing here, which was a sad commentary on the Casino Node. He was a retrofitted servant unit liveried in pinstripes and white gloves, with an aquiline nose that spoke of good breeding. I could have kept my backup mods in a traditional terminal, but I was lonely enough to convince myself that the bot provided a human touch. I held off from the depressing realization that Denholm was probably my best friend at this point.

I grabbed my swipe stick for the maglev snake. The tool was no larger than a hypodermic needle, but it reminded me to ask Denholm a question. He turned to me, regarding me with his frozen features that made him seem like a statue in a wax museum.

"What is he offering?"

"Five thousand dark," Denholm responded in his posh accent. "And fifty in credit."

I smiled. "Wonderful, that means I can beat the cap and take two baths per day for the month."

Denholm bowed obeisantly. "Very good, sir." I glanced back toward the closet. "Can I pack my bullpup?"

My butler friend shook his head. "No sir, Mr. Blankstone requests your presence at the Schengen Palace and only select private security officers and police may carry or conceal."

"Damn." My chipped clearance allowed me to get into most places with little trouble, but I would have to go relatively naked to meet the starchitect/mega-developer. His name was on almost everything in the Schengen, practically down to the last roll of toilet paper. "Take the night off," I said, before leaving.

I walked down the hotel corridor, which was empty save for a couple of low-rolling marks walking in swimsuits and flip-flops toward the Riviera. They would amuse themselves there by stepping into giant, human-sized hamster balls spinning against each other on a manmade lake.

"I can't wait to see the volcano!" One half of the twosome passing me said. That's how I knew they were tourists. No native liked the volcano, except from a distance. It was easy to admire the pulsing and ruby tones of the thing as it smoldered and tendrils of dry ice spilled upward. Once it erupted onto itself though, there was no amount of scented freshener or dye that could keep those in the know from thinking about the truth. While the volcano was distracting one's eye, it was also busy purifying "night water." All the liquid waste from the Schengen- including all the expelled Mai Tai's and Mojitos from those in the Casino Node- was being filtrated and cleaned for recycling; it was best not to think about it.

I stepped into the elevator, pressed the "Ground" button, and subvoc'd to Denholm. "Please remove the top of your head by the time I'm home."

There was a slight delay, and then the answer, "Yes sir."

The request was mildly odd, but I preferred to occasionally gaze into the transparent bubble casing shielding all that info and memory inside the butler bot's head. It functioned as a kind of night light for me, a glowing network of circuitry inside a luminous snow globe.

The elevator brought me down to the ground floor, and I stepped out into the lobby. Baubles from the zirconia chandeliers above reflected in the polished marble tiles underfoot. The sound of slots paying off chimed and buzzed behind me. I walked past the chiseled busts of the Caesars arranged in the entryway, passing through the ever-revolving brass door out into the muggy night.

I hadn't bothered to check with reception to see if one of the fixed wing jobs on the roof was juiced. I actually needed a little bit of time to walk and think. I wouldn't have been able to do that while in one of the sky slicers.

"Blankstone, Bernard," I said.

The man was a big enough whale for autocomplete to kick in after the first two syllables. I walked toward the nearest snake station, which ran through another faux Alexandrian temple. A steel maglev flew soundlessly past the somber gray porticos of the terminal and my ping report came back to me.

I muted my enhanced-reality mod with a slight grinding of the molars since I needed to see, but not before getting a quick glimpse of my potential client. He had sharp features and severe lines etched into his bronzed skin, which must have been exfoliated with products that cost more than a night with the average free walking femme. His nose brought to mind birds of prey, and the eyes were as impassive as those of the Caesars that watched me on my daily treks down the Zhakpot's hallways.

A honeyed female voice informed me that Blankstone had been born to the silver spoon set. His father was a famed British fashion designer who got his start as a humble haberdasher. Bernard Senior had wisely invested his money in a water-soluble polyvinyl alcohol that would come to play a major role in the dissolvable laundry sachet revolution.

So far it was not riveting reading. I pulled my wand from my clamshell jacket and flashed it at the turnstile. I shuffled onto the steel snake and took my place on an egg-shaped Bauhaus chair whose interior was made of ribbed leather. I could never score one of those things during the day.

"Your stop is eight stations away," Denholm said.

"Thank you sir." I had subvoc'd my response. People were used to seeing each other talk to themselves during the day, but schizophrenia was as likely as sub-vocalization on the snake at night.

The train pulled out. I enjoyed the sonorous whirring, the barely audible hum. I closed my eyes for a moment, placed my wand back into one of the many zippered pouches on my clamshell, and I listened to the rest of the report.

I learned about Blankstone's failed art gallery. He'd had a disastrous prenuptial-less first marriage that cost him a large portion of his trust fund and probably soured him on love for the rest of his life. The marriage did produce issue, though. There was a daughter named Matina Stovis (she had taken her husband's name) who now worked for an NGO and was rumored to have her fair share of daddy issues according to the few tabloid-style items that made it through the ping's auto-sifter.

The snake stopped. It discharged some passengers, while a few others got on. The report then informed me that Bernard Junior decided apropos of nothing to sell his entire share of CleanSafe (the first company to hold patent rights on the detergent his father invested in) before disappearing for a few years.

The record went blank, and I grew curious. There was no square inch on our mapped earth where even a sewer rat could hide without being tracked. I asked myself how the hell someone with Blankstone's pedigree could disappear.

The glow of a homeless man seated across from me drew me out of my thoughts. He had apparently been sleeping in Loomoo Park, and had cozied up to rest beneath one of the bioluminescent ferns or bushes. The front of his paper-thin duster jacket was splotched with violet and aquamarine like the markings of a tropical fish.

I didn't have to worry about my wand with him, since it was programmed to pulse and shock anyone whose thumbprint didn't match mine. I hazarded from the smell of muscatel on his breath that our friend didn't have hacking on his agenda, at least not of the computer kind. There were a few reported incidents of violence on the maglev weekly, although most of that was suicides flinging themselves in front of the snake. It took the bots less than two minutes to scrape a carcass up at this point, which was still too much of an inconvenience for many of the Schengen's busier residents.

The train lurched and stopped again. The woman in my ear announced that after Bernard Blankstone emerged from his self-imposed exile, he took a junior position at an architectural firm. He gained admittance first on the strength of his name, which still conferred a certain cache. Soon however, Blankstone's green-friendly pagodas with the solar panels started to be all the rage. His name eventually earned its place on the exposed steel front of the architectural headquarters of Blankstone, Marcuse & Leitham. He garnered the firm praise and wealth beyond dreams of avarice, as well as no small surfeit of tradeable energy credits.

When questioned about his previous sabbatical, Blankstone always remained mum. Asked about his architectural abilities, he always maintained that he was an autodidact. He claimed he read books on the subject to build a foundation, and perused journals to stay current. It was almost de rigeur for someone from his station in life to be modded or chipped, but Bernard grew indignant and stood firm when asked if he was enhanced. He maintained that he had learned everything the hard way, bricks and mortar-style.

A cyber-psychological examination confirmed that Bernard was all meat, which was more than I could say for myself. I had lost my arm to a stickup kid's shotgun and it wasn't as if I had much choice.

I stroked the myomar covering my left arm, down to the steel joint of the elbow. It was an old model they no longer grew in biotanks. I had developed a fondness for the appendage that bordered on affection. I was in Kitsch Central living in the Zhakpot, and I had no qualms about seeing myself as partially constituted of vintage parts.

The snake stopped, and Loomoo Park glowed ahead of me. The treetops radiated gold and blue, pulsing like jellyfish. Their colors bled together into one soft rainbow. A glass-skinned structure across the street caught light from the park, each of its panes looking like liquid color displays. The stories of the building moved upward in progressively smaller glass boxes, so that it gave the appearance of a crystal ziggurat. The building's top cube ascended high enough into the night to look like it was touching the moon. A few tiny figures moved along the observation deck above me, no doubt taking in the view of the adjacent nodes. Bombayberg was to the north and Muscovite Central was to the south. I got off the train.

My destination was straight ahead, inside of Schengen Palace. I walked forward, my feet touching soft red carpet that had been rolled out for some sort of gala event that was already underway. I hadn't bothered to ping for Blankstone's voice, although it was dubious that I could have recorded it. Anyone worth as much as him had proprietary blocks to keep his audio info under lock and key. Nevertheless, something told me that the voice echoing through the glass palace was his.

The acoustics were crystal clear, and his boilerplate about "synergy" and "our dynamic future" almost sounded original when powered by such a strong microphone. Two heavies with cinderblock-shaped heads and red cummerbunds moved toward me. One clenched his fist into a mighty anvil and I said, "John Moglich, here to see Mr. Blankstone."

The meat hook unclenched, and the jaw spasmodically pulsed. "Go to the back of the auditorium and wait until the speech is over," Blockhead One whispered.

His friend didn't want to be left out of the fun, and he patted down my clamshell. "You ain't dressed for the occasion, so stay in the shadows."

"That's my specialty." I smiled, and I wasn't surprised when neither one of them smiled back at me.

Blankstone's disembodied voice followed me into the main hall. I looked up toward the stage, where he spoke with a microphone headset and gesticulated with his hands. This was my first time inside Schengen Palace. I looked around. I did my best to stay away from the crowd, which was a veritable who's-who RSVP'd from various nodes.

I spotted a familiar face in the shadows. Lieutenant Dear pulled me down toward the table where he and three other plainclothes cops sat. "Johnny," he whispered. "What the hell are you doing here?"

I sat down in the only free seat available at the table, and I pointed toward the stage to change the subject. "It's a hell of a setup."

Everything around Blankstone appeared to be made of crystal so clear that I could have sworn the yawning groin arch above the rich man on stage was hewn from one giant ice sculpture. The transparency of the building allowed me to look right past Blankstone and through the wall behind him, to an impressive biolumo graffiti mural. Kids from Bombayberg had apparently been sneaking into Loomoo Park and siphoning enough glow from the plants to draw a blue Ganesh with an array of arms, balancing on a pastel lotus that cast Blankstone's face into a pinkish hue.

"It's something," Dear whispered. He pointed to the dicks around him. "This here is John Moglich. He was department golden boy back in the day." He clenched my left arm, felt the cyber-mod he'd forgotten until this moment, and then released. "We were on meat beat together." He lightly touched his salt and pepper toothbrush moustache, and then ran the same hand over his flattop so fast I was surprised he didn't get a papercut.

I looked at the table in front of us. I saw synth lobsters, but no drinks. That meant they probably weren't here as guests. Dear didn't miss anything. "That's right. We got some reports of death threats, and we're checking it out."

I looked up toward the stage. Blankstone was still droning. "Who the hell would want to kill him?"

Dear didn't shrug, which meant he had his own ideas and wasn't sharing. I think he was sharp enough to realize I wasn't going to spill anything, either. He was also kind enough not to bust my balls by mentioning I now made a living tracking down lost towels at the Zhakpot.

Dear's star was on the rise. I'd given Denholm instructions to update me whenever my old detective buddy's name came up on a news screamer. My butler had shortly thereafter informed me that Lieutenant Dear's squad had recently busted up a cartel operating near the Edge who'd been growing synth opiates in yeast cultures. His task force had unearthed enough to OD the whole Schengen, apparently.

The Edge was now the subject on stage. "Solid waste byproduct analysis from illegal coal combustion shows that without our present defenses, the Schengen would be dealing with over one-billion tons of coal ash slurry per year."

Dear leaned toward me, and his fork clanked against his plate. "Every rich man thinks he's a genius and a hero."

A woman among the quality seated in front of us shifted in her chair, and her high black organza wrap and batwing crape epaulettes masked my view of the stage. Most everyone else aside from Ms. Lunar Eclipse seemed to be tastefully dressed. Illusion wear was scant and muted to dull boa-constrictor camo patterns. Those who wore fi-op diodes made sure their emitters were muted to an icy blue that complimented rather than took away from the beauty of the Palace.

13

None of the men seemed to be wearing compression fabrics. If one was wealthy enough apparently, they didn't have to hide their gut or feel shame. "The phasing project," Blankstone said, "that is, our philanthropic attempt to implement a program that might somehow…" He faltered, and then resumed, "incorporate the Edge into the greater Nodes has been the goal that ever recedes to the horizon when we attempt to seize it." Bernard Blankstone reached his hand out into the ether, and clutched empty air to counterpoint his statement.

Dear rolled his eyes. "But we should remember not to cast aspersions on those in the Edge before looking closer to home." He gazed out onto the shadowed crowd. "As I'm sure most of you are aware, only one of the Nodes has achieved a platinum sustainability rating. This means…"

Blankstone coughed, searched the stage for water. An underling appeared from stage left, sporting a polka-dotted bowtie colorful as a parakeet. He handed Blankstone a small bottle of sparkling mineral water. The starchitect-developer incorporated the awkward interruption into his presentation, thinking on the fly as he held the glass bottle aloft. "Water," he said, "the source of all life."

Dear muttered to me like a ventriloquist, through clenched teeth. "Tell 'em about your shit volcano." The other detectives at the table caught his sotto vocce dig, and grunted loud enough to get the woman in widow gear ahead of me to turn her giant headpiece around.

She glared, but her anger at least caused her to move enough to give me a direct line of sight to Blankstone. What I saw was not something I expected to see. Blankstone wasn't invigorated by the small ripple of laughter that followed his joke. Instead he seemed to lose not only of his confidence, but his very motor bearings. He dropped the glass bottle to the stage apron, where it shattered into shards and fizzled.

He clutched his throat as if poisoned, and I made a mental note to check the face of the boy with the bowtie against those in my internal mugshot feed. The theory that the kid from stage-left had a hand in his poisoning (or whatever it was) got blown to shreds in the next moment, as the boy quickly ran to the billionaire's side. I subvoc'd a *Record* directive for my mod. I sensed as I did so that something of note was happening, but that I might not be able to process it all in real time and that I might want to go back later to review it.

Blankstone was in so much pain that he could only thrash and kick his feet. The wind-milling of his arms caught the nearby boy on the point of his jaw, knocking him out cold. Blankstone didn't appear to pack much of a punch, so I figured he must have been in a terrible panic to hit so hard and that he had been given extra strength by his hysteria.

Everyone at my table stood, Dear scraping his chair as he scanned the room with his hawk eyes. Guests muttered and whispered in confusion, which somewhat settled as Blankstone appeared to recover for a moment. He stood before us beneath the acoustical shell of the stage. He opened his mouth. His tongue fell out of his head, landing on the floor with a thick, wet slap.

A woman in front of me fainted and landed face-first on the table in front of her. She pulled the white cloth, silverware, and glasses onto the ground with her like a novice magician who'd botched the oldest trick in the book.

"Denholm," I subvoc'd.

"Yes sir?"

"I'm recording this, but I need a backup just in case I lose it. Double up on anything I'm seeing and store it until I get home."

"Yes sir."

Thick blood poured from Blankstone's mouth. He attempted to speak, and the red became a stream of projectile vomit that lurched over the crowd and caused a horrified gasp to echo over the crystal walls.

I looked toward the stage. I saw the tongue slithering between the crushing stampede of feet making their way toward the exits and clogging the doors. It moved on its own and left a trail of slime like a fat-bellied garden slug.

"What the fuck?" Dear saw it, too.

We and the other detectives remained crouched near our table. We weren't cowardly enough to do the mad dash like everyone else, but at the same time a tongue moving of its own volition- while a plausible enough mod in itself - was a lot scarier than a drug dealer from the Edge shooting at you.

"I don't think it's alive," I said. "I think it's programmed."

Blankstone was now in an immobile heap on the stage, crumpled over like a ragdoll. I hoped he was dead, for his sake. If Dear sweated any harder I could have seen my reflection in his beads of perspiration. "Whatever it was," he said, "it had *eyes* and its own mouth."

A tongue with a mouth and eyes was too much, but thankfully consciousness wasn't on the agenda and I wouldn't have to think about it anymore. There was a loud explosion. The icy crystals of the Schengen Palace fissured and cracked, seams appearing in the lancet windows. Tables overturned and I was lifted off my feet, into darkness and sleep

CHAPTER TWO

AFTERMATH

They were seeding the clouds above the Green Node for rain. That meant the grass roofs in that part of town would be fed, but it also meant the beaten Cordoba domes in the Muscovite Zone were weeping golden rust. Denholm had warned me beforehand, and I'd taken an umbrella. Now I was walking along the granite embankment by the riverside, killing time until my appointment in the mod shop.

No one aside from Blankstone had been killed in the blast, but maybe that was the point. Walking usually helped me think, but so far my little jaunt hadn't helped me begin to answer why Blankstone had called me earlier requesting my presence, or why exactly he had been offed. None of this was my job, I knew. The circumscribed limits of my world were the Zhakpot, and that was the way I liked it.

Rain pelted the fabric of my umbrella with the force of hail, and I counted the ship mooring rings that had been fixed in the embankment on my right. They looked to be spaced equally distant from each other. Each of the brass rings was nestled in the mouths of stone lions, giving them the appearance of door knockers.

The sky was overcast, and the old ironwork streetlamps glowed through the fog. I glanced back in the direction of Muscovite Med, subvoc'd my enhanced reality, and got a readout in front of my vision of the mod shop's hours and ratings. They were still closed. I turned the enhancement off, coughed into my closed fist, and continued on with my saunter.

"Moglich!"

I turned, expecting either a fist or a bullet from the way my name had been called. It was only Lieutenant Dear, wearing a black raincoat. He walked toward me. I stood in place to make his job easier. "I thought once you got those bars, you became a desk jockey. What brings you to this Node?"

He ignored my dig and my question, which meant he really had something on his mind. "I know you," he said.

"I know that," I replied.

Dear rolled his eyes. "You know what I mean. I know you well enough to know you recorded what went down at the Schengen Palace."

"You on that case?"

"The whole city's on that fucking case."

"That thing that crawled out of Blankstone's mouth," I said, "whatever it was, a mod of some kind or bioengineered parasite..."

"Yeah?" Dear said. His eyes were wide and his mouth was open. The rain came down harder.

"What was it?"

"It was explosive, whatever it was. It detonated and it took Blankstone's head with it."

I looked down at my walking shoes, made of synth leather. I sighed. I had been dreaming about that tongue with its own set of eyes and mouth, and I was hoping to give a name to the nightmare in the hopes its power would ebb. Dear had no answers though, which meant the thing's power would grow in my sleep. None of the whale songs or cresting foam sound effects Denholm emitted at night would make my dreams any easier.

"Did you record the event?" Dear asked.

"Yeah."

He exhaled. The relief washing over him was so strong his shoulders sagged. He thought his department was saved. It wasn't. I burst his bubble. "The second I was released from hospital quarantine, I ran the feed in my Enhanced Reality at home and..."

"And?" He cut me off.

"And I got a message. 'Digital watermark not authenticated. Error.'"

"'File not found,'" Dear said. Apparently he and his boys had gotten the same message. He shook his head, turned his collar up against the wind. "Whoever did this was not only one mean motherfucker, he or she was also quite smart."

"Or they."

"Or they," Dear repeated. His eyes narrowed. "Why were you there? I meant to ask you that."

I smiled. He didn't return the gesture. "Am I a suspect?" I asked.

"It's nothing personal. Like I said, the whole city's on this case and the whole city's suspect."

"Blankstone was a big fish," I said

"He made a lot of people rich and he made a lot of people poor. He had his hands in more pies than a fat kid playing on a baker's windowsill."

"So the perp can hack, we know that. Did he cover his tracks?"

Dear nodded. "Not a single digital footprint."

A lead-gray seeding dirigible drifted through the cloudy ether on the horizon. I turned back in the direction of Muscovite Med, and started walking. My old friend followed at my side. "What are you doing in Ruskieville, anyway?"

I pointed toward the clinic, which was housed in a colorless Gropius block that looked like a Soviet barracks. It was next to Czarina's, a Faberge gallery whose façade revealed bronze Valkyries holding up gilded Easter eggs stained green, blue, and red. "The hospital said I just had a few cuts after the blast, and quarantine revealed no chemical or biological agents in that tongue thing that blew up. I still got to get my mods checked to make sure everything's in working order, though."

We waited for a couple of bubbletop cruisers to float across the cobblestone street in front of us, and I coughed on a whiff of ethanol. It was time to come clean. Blankstone had never been my client, just a potential one. On top of that, he was dead and thus there was no reason to hold back with an old friend. I also thought that if I was nice to Dear that maybe he would play nice with me.

"I was in the Zhakpot minding my own business, when Denholm told me I had an incoming from Blankstone. Bernard had requested my presence at the Palace."

Dear nodded and we crossed the street. "Sounds good. Who's Denholm, though?"

"A house butler unit at the Zhakpot, an old world antique. I modded him to be a backup." I paused, a little embarrassed. "He's also a friend."

Dear was too distracted to judge. He glanced through the frosted glass window of Czarina's at the eggs on their pedestals. "Shit, one of those is worth more than I make in a decade."

"I don't know what to tell you," I said. "Start taking bribes."

He grinned at that. "Too late. I'm off Vice. Dope is where the money is."

"That and Faberge eggs." I turned toward the front door of Muscovite Med when I thought of something and turned around. The heavy downpour had slackened to a light pelting drizzle. "So you guys are really at square one on this thing?"

"Not quite," Dear said, cryptically. He waited. Time was a luxury I didn't have right now. I had an appointment.

"Don't keep me in suspense, old buddy."

Lieutenant Dear held his hands out, cupping them for rain as if accepting an offering of holy water. He splashed the rainwater in his face and shook his head from side to side like a dog. "Blankstone shit his pants when his head exploded."

"Can't say I blame him," I said.

"Naturally, we sent the feces to lab for analysis."

"And?"

"And…" He hesitated, and this time I could tell it wasn't because he was being cagey or didn't want to share. It was that he had a hard time either believing or understanding whatever it was he had to impart. "His shit had prolactin in it."

I had a GenMed mod that I could have checked for an explanation of what that was, but I thought it would be impolite to space out into research mode with a friend right there in front of me. On top of that I wasn't sure if the mod still worked after the blast at Schengen Palace. Someone with the skillset to pull a digital watermark spoof probably also knew how to chase his explosive with a pulse bomb to EMP the hell out of my hardware. We'd find out soon enough. My arm hadn't been going spastic, so we knew my cyberware was in order.

"Prolactin is what's produced in breastmilk. It's considered a 'mothering hormone.' They shoot it into rats that never had kids, and all of a sudden they're giving a brood of baby rats tender loving care."

I thought of something. "Did you check Blankstone's bits and pieces, the family jewels?"

"We did a full autopsy." Dear's spine went ramrod straight. He apparently didn't like his methods being questioned.

"I only ask because I thought maybe he had a tranny mod, or he was getting transition boosters. Who knows?"

He shook his head. "We thought of that. He was all man. No breast implants, no estrogen boosters."

"Weird."

"It gets weirder."

I waited for him to tell me how. "We also found traces of colostrum." He knew I didn't know what that meant without checking my med mod, so he said, "It's produced in the alveoli of a woman's breasts where milk is made." He laughed, more in disbelief than in amusement. "This is probably the first time I've interviewed a lactation consultant on a case."

"Why are you doing the interviewing? You fought tooth and nail to be a Louie. Those golden bars should keep you out of the trenches."

"This case is too interesting for me to sit back and let all the dicks beat feet."

"It's certainly different," I allowed. "So, what did your breastmilk contact tell you about this stuff?"

"The colostrum?" Dear asked. He was catching a cold, despite the heavy raincoat.

"Yeah."

"It's basically liquid gold for the baby."

I had a eureka moment strong enough for me to snap my fingers. "Maybe Blankstone's girlfriend was pregnant."

He shook his head. He and the department had been down this road and apparently scratched that idea from the list. "Maybe..." Here I was grasping. "Maybe he's got a mistress and she's pregnant. Could be a fetish?" Perhaps he had a lactation thing. From the little info I'd garnered about Blankstone on my ride on the maglev toward the Palace, I thought it would make sense. Someone who eschewed mods and preferred to learn the bricks and mortar way might also be the kind of guy who preferred suckling breastmilk to sucking silicone.

"Anyway," Dear said, bringing me out of my thoughts. He apparently didn't feel like standing out in the cold and the rain while the gears worked in my mind. "If you find something out, let us know. Help us with the investigation, I mean."

"I'm not on this case," I said.

"Yeah, but this case might be on you. You got called to Schengen Palace for some reason."

"Yeah, to meet with a guy who's dead. It sounds like my part in this drama has been played."

"Maybe," Dear said. I didn't like that word. *Maybe* was ambivalent, complicated. I wanted to get back to the ease of the Zhakpot, of using my infrared and x-ray mods to spot cheaters on the gaming floor of the casino. I wanted to get back to getting comped meals, free plays, and drinks for myself. I already missed the hours spent in the swimming pool or staring out the window of my thirtieth floor room, watching the rubes climb the steel skeleton of the Eifel Tower. *Maybe* was a headache I definitely didn't need.

Dear patted me on my shoulder, the meat one, and then turned. "Let me know if you hear anything."

"Will do." I turned away from him, and opened the door to Muscovite Med. Time for a checkup.

CHAPTER THREE

TESTING THE ARM

The Stalinist décor inside of the building was as grim as that of the outer shell. The walls were a sickly mint, and it was easy for me to imagine the tiles splattered with blood from a sadistic dentist's interrogation gone awry. I had been in Doctor Stapleton's office numerous times, and I had never seen the man. He worked remotely, and for all I knew he was performing his work in boxer shorts and leg garters from his living room. Sometimes he coughed in a way that made me imagine he was a heavy smoker.

"Okay, Mr. Moglich, you said you had some concerns about your mods?" His scanning tool whirred and hovered toward me. It was made of brushed chrome and shaped like a brain, sans convolutions. I always felt queasy as the thing drifted toward me, as if it might be an alien yearning to take a bite out of me or it might emit a ray that could give me cancer.

"Yes, I was in a blast."

"The one at Schengen Palace?" Dr. Stapleton's voice came from the grey steel brain before me.

"That's the one." I leaned back in the banana-shaped Naugahyde recliner.

The machine *tut-tutted*. "That was a terrible attack on a good man. Dr. Blankstone was a true humanitarian."

"'Doctor' Blankstone?"

The voice in the machine qualified itself, coughed. "Dr. Blankstone received an honorary degree from my alma mater."

"I see." The room was windowless, but my sixth sense told me the rain had stopped outside.

"Okay, Mr. Moglich. We're going to do an implant check, and then an on-site attendant is going to check your prosthesis. Sound good?"

I nodded, but I didn't know whether or not he had seen it. "Sounds good," I said. I was nervous, as I always was when my life was in someone else's hands.

"I'm going to speak to you now." A red light flickered from the steel chassis squatting in front of me, and I grew even more unsettled as the thought flitted through my mind that it was a laser sight on a weapon scope.

"Okay."

"Gentleman Jim Corbett fought the other fellow to a draw. What language was that?"

"English," I replied.

"Susie took the dog for an evening constitutional."

"English again," I said.

"The doctor thinks I might have a hernia."

"English."

The red light segued to an icy blue ray. "Okay, Mr. Moglich. Your Babel implant is working just fine."

I sat up on the reclining chair. "Just out of curiosity, what languages were you speaking?"

"Hebrew, Japanese, and Arabic." I laughed. "Amazing, isn't it?" The doctor asked, from wherever he was. "You achieve a greater degree of fluency with something the size of a hair follicle being installed in ten minutes than you would with two decades of constant practice."

"I guess it's cheating."

"It's not cheating if everyone does it," the doctor said, and I wondered if he acquired his skills the easy way. "It's important to remember that not everyone has the constitution to handle these implants, both software mods and hardware." His voice grew stilted, and I could tell he was reading something as he spoke to me. "Your brass at the Schengen PD must have thought quite highly of you to recommend you for these implants so early in your career."

The fluorescent lights were too strong for him to see me blushing slightly. "If everyone handled their implants as well as you, cyberpsychosis would be nothing but an urban legend."

"It's real enough alright," I said. I'd spent quite a bit of time on patrol putting down men who'd allowed their hardware and jacks to do their thinking for them, men who ended up literally strangled by their own hand in some cases.

"On the subject of cyberpsychosis," Doctor Stapleton said, "are you getting subvoc echoes?"

"I don't think so."

"Good. There's nothing worse than getting an incoming message and mistaking it for a voice in your head."

"Except for hearing a voice in your head and mistaking it for an incoming message," I said, joking.

"Both have been known to happen from time to time, but you seem to keep your head on a swivel."

The door to the examination room opened, and a squat refugee from the Edge stepped into the room. The doctor took note of him and said, "Now let's make sure we've got that arm on a swivel, too."

I turned to the little brown man whose face was a reconstructed putty of flesh torn apart by something like napalm. Doing cyberpsychosis tests was dangerous, but work was scarce for those few from the Edge who immigrated into one of the main Nodes. They knew that being expendable was still better than being hunted.

The man held a length of rebar in his hand, which he set down next to a sink by the wall operated by a foot treadle. He had a soup bowl haircut and white streaks in his black hair, and the scars from whatever hit his face worked their way in a crosshatched grid down his arms in a pattern as solid as fish scales.

He looked at the machine looking at me. "Okay, Doctor?"

"Please, Ali."

Ali reached for my left arm with the fearful respect of a snake charmer trying not to get bitten. He rotated my arm left, and looked relieved to see he was dealing with a quick-change mount. I looked at the sweaty neoprene liner of my stump.

"Lost it in a gunfight," I said, hoping that satisfied his curiosity.

He giggled, and pointed at the scars on his face. "I lost too." I had no idea what language he was speaking, since the Babel implant was working fine. He set the limb in the sink and then returned to clean the area around the thumb catch on my stump with sterilizing foam.

"So no phantom vocalizations?" The doctor asked me.

"None."

"Are you feeling a phantom limb where your arm should be?" I gazed at the stump, while the arm was soaking in a disinfectant solution in the sink. It looked strange, but it felt like nothing.

"No, I'm good."

Ali had finished cleaning my stump, and he took the still-damp mount and plugged it back in. He twisted right and there was a satisfying catch. My hand reflexively opened and closed, and Ali jumped back.

"It's alright," I said. "I've got it under control now."

"Test its power," the doctor said to Ali.

Ali picked up the rebar and held it out to me. "Grip it," the doctor said. I squeezed the metal in my hand. "Break it." I clenched my fist and the metal shattered like particle board.

"Sensory test, Ali."

The Edge refugee walked back over to the sink, grabbed a thick gauge needle from a glass container adjacent to another cylinder filled with tongue depressors. "Don't stab him too hard, but poke him pretty good."

I subvoc'd a command to the left arm to turn off its sensors, and it was as if the limb was still removed. Yet I could see Ali pressing the vat-grown flesh of my arm hard enough with his needle to pierce the skin.

"Do you feel anything?" the doctor asked.

"Nothing," I said. "Everything is in working order."

"Good," the doctor said, and then to the aide, "Thank you, Ali."

The man bowed, disposed of the needle, and picked up the two severed pieces of rebar. He left without another word. I looked at the chrome monster bearing down on me. I caught my reflection, which was something I usually avoided doing. I saw my impassive face, the pain so deep and total that I refused to let it surface most of the time.

My hair had gone grey after three years on the force, cotton-white after five. I had never bothered to dye it. I had no desire to try hair plugs, despite my other implants.

I thought the doctor and I were about done, but he spoke. "Have you been working on your cursive?" I felt like lying, but I didn't know what kind of vitals he could monitor with the device currently bearing down on me. Men rarely beat machines at lie detection these days, so I came clean.

"Remind me again why I'm supposed to be doing that?" Graphite and real paper were expensive. I could have worked a stylus on an LCD screen, but I'd been told I wouldn't get the full effect that way.

The doctor exhaled, and I could tell from the tone in his voice that he was pissed with me for the first time that day. It had all been going so well up until now. "It helps your brain stay functionally specialized. It helps with movement, control, and thinking. Look at this kind of co-activation as a way to keep your mods clean and separate, sort of like when you polish a gun."

"Gotcha." I appreciated that he was tailoring his similes for an ex-law enforcement officer. What I couldn't tell him was that I had spent so much time on the force that Dear and the rest of the boys had imprinted some kind of "pussy" mod into me during all those towel slapping sessions in the showers and locker rooms. The second I sat down with Denholm at my side and I wrote my curlicue letters, I would see the old squad in my mind's eye. *Get a load of Moglich! The guy used to be able to hawk a kid with twin mod legs across a roof and dodge bullets without breaking a sweat. Now he's playing security guard at the Zhakpot in return for the free buffet and his little boy toy. They practice their cursive together in their downtime.*

I sat up in the chair, and promised to work on my cursive to keep my mods from melting into one another. I thought of something and stretched back out. "Doc, can you check one more thing?"

"It's your time," he said, through the machine.

"I recorded something at the Schengen Palace, and whenever I try to check it-"

"You get a message that says 'Digital Watermark cannot be authenticated' or words to that effect. Correct?"

The wind left my lungs. "I guess everyone got tagged with the same EMP."

"I almost got 'tagged' as you put it."

That made me sit back up again. "How do you mean?"

"That pulse was chased with a virus," the doctor said. "When I tried to investigate the spoof, the little machine you're looking at had to shut down as a failsafe. If it had kept running, it would have been overloaded with Direct Denial of Service attacks."

I rubbed my stubble with my right hand and thought, or tried to think. "Whoever hit Blankstone knew what he was doing."

The doctor's steel brain contraption lifted from the bed, and moved to the other side of the room where it folded onto itself like the crane arm of a cherry picker. The doctor's voice came from the machine one last time. "Whoever killed Bernard Blankstone is smarter than any mod can make a man."

"You could be right," I said.

The shining steel brain went dormant, and I sat up in the chair. The Naugahyde cringed beneath me as I stood and donned my jacket. I walked toward the lobby and removed my sticker from the outer pocket of my clamshell. The nurse was another Edger who'd made it through the pollution and bullets to partake of the relatively good life in the Nodes.

I waved my wand over hers, and waited for the LED to pulse green. "Thank you, Mr. Moglich."

"Thank you, ma'am." She was attractive, with a pert nose and a red bob haircut. A jagged bolt of lust moved through me, but I ignored it. I hadn't slept with a woman in years, and with all the troubles in my heart and mind I wasn't sure if I could get it up without a priapic implant. I wasn't letting any back-alley butcher get near my dick, either.

I walked outside and looked across the slate embankment. The river coursed in chopping waves black and shiny as crude oil. Ottoman spires and pointed minarets rose toward the vanishing point on the horizon. I was ready to go home and try my cursive, but a beautiful woman stood in my way.

She stepped toward me, ascending the steps of Muscovite Med. "Detective Moglich?" It felt like no one had called me that in a long time, at least no one who looked like her.

CHAPTER FOUR

SOME MEMORIES STILL WORK

My cached stash of recent recordings may have failed me, but it didn't take me long to place the woman who approached me on the steps of Muscovite Med. I stared at her and let it come back to me. She was of indeterminate Asian extraction, perhaps Hawaiian and Japanese, or Thai and Chinese. Whatever the combination, the mixture of mom's and dad's genes had worked. She had sedate brown eyes, their intelligence highlighted by tortoise shell glasses whose frames sat on her high cheekbones. Her features were sharp and narrow, with a severe, almost cruel sex appeal inherent in them. White women tortured themselves in tanning beds trying to get her tone, a soft tan with a high natural gleam matched by the shine of her raven hair. I choked trying to stifle my reaction to her beauty.

"Do you remember me?" She asked. I brought up my enhanced reality mod and cycled through recorded files, and the feed appeared before my eyes. I always made sure to remain stationary whenever I reviewed a feed on foot, since I didn't want to walk in front of a Maglev train while reliving a recorded memory.

I was walking down the carpeted hall of the Zhakpot, when I heard light weeping and the dull sounds of a scuffle from one of the boardrooms. I ducked into the ballroom to find an exec with a disheveled tie wrestling a woman onto the varnished surface of a conference table. Her stockings rustled and she grunted as she attempted to pull the buttons from his dress shirt.

I left the memory. "Tia Mifune," I said, looking at her.

"Thank you for saving me," she said.

"I was just making my rounds," I replied. "Whatever happened to him?" I asked, of the potential rapist. I'd bound him with flexi-cuffs and turned him in to hotel management, who then presumably turned him over to SPD.

"Nothing," she said, and her tightened features grew tauter. "He had diplomatic immunity and he was out of the country by morning."

"I'm sorry."

"Don't be," she said. "You did what you were supposed to do."

Her dark eyes glowed like amber, and I tried to change the subject. I didn't want to make her relive the trauma, or further mull over the injustice of what had happened that night in the Zhakpot. "So what have you been up to?"

She subvoc'd something to my enhanced reality mod, and I accepted the incoming. I was pretty sure she didn't come to the steps of Muscovite Med to give me a virus or to spoof me for her own ends.

I read her CV. She held degrees in myofascial and shiatsu massage. She was the founder and CEO of Touch LLC, a company created to provide fully-clothed, platonic hugs and caresses to the loneliest members of Schengen City's population. She spoke to compliment the readout as it scrolled in front of my eyes. "All are welcome," she said. "Your weight, gender, occupation, race, religion, and age are of no concern. All human beings deserve to be touched."

"I see." I didn't necessarily disagree. It had been years since I had been touched by a woman or touched one.

"We deal especially with the widows and widowers, and the disabled."

"Is it lucrative?"

Her facial muscles twitched, and I was afraid I'd offended her. "I would say it's more rewarding than lucrative, but it does pay the bills."

It looked like it, I thought. I studied her outfit, a tweed blazer pulled tightly over a steel-bone corset. The top of the corset was shaped like a heart. The two halves of the heart shape brought her coconut-colored breasts into tightly defined, ample cleavage. The jacket met a knee-length skirt made of upcycled material that looked like shagreened fish scale leather reclaimed from the once-poisonous port waters.

I killed my ER mod and asked, "So, how may I help you?"

"Are you available?" She pulled her sticker wand from a pocket on her tweed vest and held it up to me. It was green with dark coin and credits. "I would like to pay you five-thousand and fifty in energy, if you'd be willing to accompany me back to the Ming."

The platonic touching game must have been paying well, if she was willing to offer so much and she lived somewhere as posh as the Ming. Zhakpot paid me a thousand a week, and twenty in credits per month. I also got free use of their exercise and spa facilities, and comped meals.

"I'm available."

She turned. "Walk with me." She moved quickly for someone whose heels had such high stilettos.

I walked until I was alongside her. She brandished her credit sticker in her right hand like a dagger, and I pulled my own credit wand from the zippered pouch of my clamshell. I held my wand out to hers and she waved, transferring five-thousand instantly as promised.

"Thank you," I said. She ignored me, or at least didn't bother to look at me as she made her way toward the nearest maglev snake station.

"Can we discuss in public what you want me to do?"

"No," Tia said. Her nostrils flared. "And I'm not comfortable publicly subvoc'ing."

It would have to wait for the Ming, then. Dead air disturbed me, so I attempted idle chitchat as we made our way toward the station. "Tell me more about Touch, then."

I had meant her firm, but she apparently took my question to be about the noun in general. This problem wouldn't have come up with subvoc since she would have seen "Touch" capitalized as the message came in.

"It's important to the central nervous system. The bottom line is that people who are touched end up living longer, more fulfilling lives." Three Edge migrants and a teenager who'd had his face sculpted to look like an African tribal mask waited at the station. All pretended not to be fazed by her beauty.

"Caresses slow the heartrate, decrease blood pressure." She stuck her wand back into her tweed blazer. I suspected she had self-defense down to a science after her encounter at the Zhakpot, but it still wasn't smart to go waving one's wand around too much in public. "You diminish your stress hormones and increase the number of immune cells in your body with touch."

"Maybe I should pay for a session or two, then."

She looked at me, and her eyes softened. "What's your meat percentage?"

Higher than that kid with the metal mask face, I wanted to say but I tried not to start fights or insult people too close to snake tracks. "Eighty percent." I gripped my recently cleaned arm, which still reeked of sanitation foam.

"But I didn't have a choice. I got this on the force."

She glanced at the appendage. "It came in handy that night at the conference room," she said, her voice softened by genuine gratitude. I had almost crushed the larynx of the grabby businessman with diplomatic immunity that day. It was probably a good thing that I didn't kill him. If he had enough juice to dodge sexual assault charges for something that had been recorded, he could have probably gotten me bounced from my gig as house detective at the Zhakpot with one quick call.

The nickel-plated dragon's head with the forked tongue of anodized steel barreled toward us on the tracks. The dragon's body stopped on the tracks and the doors to the maglev train opened with a steamy hiss. It was headed toward Chinatown. We got onboard.

The train was packed with midday commuters, cubicle jockeys and coffin drones dressed in indistinguishable black suits with white shirts. The doors closed and I gripped a railcar pole. Tia Mifune gripped the same pole, lightly grazing my hand with her warm fingers that tapered in manicured nails. Blood rushed through my body and the hairs on the back of my neck stood on end. I exhaled, and tried to stow the rising erection. It was my first in a long time.

I asked another question to pull myself out of my thoughts. "So how did you get into this kind of work?" There was no mod that could give a man total insight into the nature of women. I still knew from my time on the force that sexually traumatizing experiences usually drove people away from touch, not toward the desire for more tactile experience.

The maglev hummed and pulled its way toward Chinatown. "I worked as an acupuncturist." She pointed with the hand not gripping the pole back in the direction of the Casino Node. "That's why I was at that conference when you found me, attending a seminar on acupuncture." I nodded. "A friend of mine taught me about therapeutic touch. She said lightly grazing people's skin with the fingers could get muscles to unclench and cause cortisol levels to drop." She clutched the pole with both hands now and said, "I know some people are needle-phobic, so I started researching the subject for myself."

I was content to listen to her, but she suddenly stopped talking and cocked her head with a quizzical expression written on her face. "Do you have a vision mod?"

"Yeah but the mod relay is a wearable contact lens, not an implant. I keep it at home and use it for forensics as the need arises."

I didn't tell her that I kept it over Denholm's eye, and that letting him wear it was a good way to keep it out of the hands of any maids with sticky fingers. Those things were expensive.

"You should wear it sometimes and study the skin."

"Do you do that?" I asked. Blighted tenements and temporary trailers for laborers appeared through the windows outside the snake. A mech sweeper the size of a building moved through a squatters' village of single-man coffin sleeping units. I could barely make out the pilot lodged inside of the metal-framed exoskeleton. He worked his joystick and caused the arms of his steel giant to crush the tiny homes, which I hoped were empty when he cubed them.

Tia brought my eyes away from the state-sanctioned carnage going on at the periphery. "I've studied the skin about as closely as one can." I was frankly afraid to use my vision lens on epidermis for that reason. To see myself or someone else so closely might have ruined my ability to see beauty permanently. It was one thing to wake up in bed with a woman after a night of drinking and to see her hair matted to the pillow, sans makeup on her face. It would have been quite another to see thousands of mites crawling on a fiber of flesh that now looked as cracked and fissured under microscopic scrutiny as a parched desert.

"A piece of skin the size of my fingernail contains more than three million cells." She took one of her hands from the pole we both gripped and twirled a fingernail. Its high varnish reflected in the light from the sun that had snuck through the seeding clouds.

"Amazing."

"That same piece of skin contains about three-hundred sweat glands and fifty nerve endings." She placed her hand over mine. She smiled at how weak she made me. I did, too. There was no use pretending that women weren't constant reminders of magic, at least women like her.

"And that's just outside of us," she said. Her eyes had been narrow slits with lids streaked with purple paint, but they now widened to saucers. "Imagine what's going on inside."

I admired her curiosity, her own wonder at the human body. I regretted how crass my first question was, the one about how much she made doing what she did. It was clear that regardless of whatever kind of coin she was bringing in, that she did what she did out of love and fascination. I did not share her love of skin though, nor her curiosity regarding the inner workings of the human body. Nano/Microsurgeons made good bank, but there was no amount of money that would get me to take on an enhanced reality perspective in order to wend my way through a long intestine.

The dragon's head now bore down on Chinatown, passing underneath an ethanol-stained arch on which twin Koi had been scalloped in stone. On top of the arch was a copper-plated Buddha finial with a wide smile on his face and man-breasts drooping over his potbelly.

The Ming was a multi-shafted skyscraper. It shot up into the sky behind a wall that gave the luxury complex its name. The tower took on the color of a moonstone in the afterglow of the storm that recently swept the Nodes.

The train stopped and we got out at the station. I followed Tia Mifune toward I knew not what. She looked back toward me and said, "The Ming is eighty-eight stories tall." Guards in riot helmets and gunners' vests patrolled the perimeter of the building with their MGs in slings. They looked relaxed and I suspected they rarely had their skills tested, and that they'd never fired their weapons outside a training setting.

An oculus disguised as a blooming narcissus twitched in a flower bed and authenticated Tia plus one, which caused the building's door to open. One of the faceless roving guards tapped the tinted face of his helmet. "Ms. Mifune."

She ignored him, and I walked in after her. "Eighty-eight," I said, "is supposed to be a good luck number in Chinese numerology, isn't it?"

I walked into the courtyard with her, and she spoke over the low trickle of a fountain. "Do you have a mod for that?"

I suspected she knew I had a Babel Mod. It was set to run in regular background mode, so I had no idea what language she was presently speaking. The truth was that I had heard the tidbit about Chinese numerology elsewhere. "I think I learned it from a gameshow," I said.

That earned me my first and perhaps only smile from Tia Mifune. We walked past a doorman in an ill-fitting concierge jacket. "Ms. Tifune," he said, trying to mask his own crush on her. She gave him a bracing smile, and we walked through the revolving doors of the Ming Luxury Complex.

Her heels clacked on the Vitruvian marble beneath her feet. "Time for you to meet someone," she said, and we stepped onto the elevator

CHAPTER FIVE

A WOMAN AFFLICTED

A victim of an attack lay curled in the fetal position in Tia Mifune's bedroom. The bed itself was an inflatable coffin cube model, placed in a four-poster bamboo frame. A red paper lantern hung above the bed, casting a soft glow over the room and suffusing it with a warm opium den glow.

"What happened?" I walked forward.

"I don't exactly know." Tia removed her jacket. "Kyra called me from home."

I stepped closer to the woman on the bed, who was breathing heavily. The perimeter of the bed was surrounded by shiatsu massage stones, which were scattered like salt by a superstitious hand. There was a lazy Susan propped next to the wounded woman. On top of the small table there was a blue and white porcelain dim sum bowl, filled with water in which a red rag soaked like bloody wonton.

The woman moaned, and I subvoc'd a command to capture her voice in case I needed it later to filter through my larynx mod for some spoofing or social engineering. "Her full name?" I asked.

The woman turned in her agonized sleep and moaned again. I noticed she had some sort of wound above her left breasts. I started recording with my eyes, and feeding the images back to Denholm at the *Zhakpot* for storage and later review.

Tia Mifune walked until she was alongside me by the bed. She reached into the porcelain bowl for the soaked rag, and made as if to wring it. I held her off with my hand and repeated my question, only this time more forcefully to bring her back to the moment. "Her name?"

"Kyra Boxer."

"Her relationship to you?"

Tia reached her hand out, and stroked her wounded friend's locks of disheveled bottle-blond hair away from her face. "She works for me, for Touch LLC."

"A client do this to her?"

"Probably some man, although she must not have been expecting it."

"Why is that?"

"All of my employees are trained in self-defense."

Tia had cleared the hair from the woman's face, which gave me a better look at her features. Kyra wore a throwback vintage beehive hairdo that had come loose in her scuffle. She also had a mouse under each eye, the one under the left swelling enough to make me worry about hematoma. I stifled the accusatory edge I knew my next question would contain.

"Why didn't you take her to the hospital?"

"She wouldn't go. She said she'd die first. She has a hemlock mod."

It was a good thing she was unconscious then, since she wouldn't be able to will herself to be euthanized and now would have been as good a time as any. "Can she speak?" I leaned down. "Kyra?" She tossed in her sleep, but her swollen eyes didn't open and her bruised lips didn't move.

One of her pendulous white breasts slipped free from her black top, and I was tempted to look away in embarrassment. There was a red spot just above the left nipple that looked like a bite mark.

"Can you remove her shirt?"

Tia paused, and then complied. I spoke to her without taking my eyes off Kyra. "I'm going to subvoc for a moment with my partner."

She nodded.

"Denholm?"

"Yes sir?" A dry English accent penetrated my mind.

"I need you to be my remote eye for a moment."

"Yes sir."

I noticed what looked like a bruise half-obscured by Kyra's right breast. I lifted the breast and realized I was looking at a port-colored birthmark. "Check the neck, chest, the ribs, and the stomach."

"Yes sir."

I waited and pointed at Kyra's swollen, milk-white breasts. I turned to Tia. She didn't seem to expect me ask her questions, since I was engaged with Denholm. "Is she pregnant?"

Tia pointed to her friend's flat stomach, complete with washboard abs

36

hard as the stones she'd scattered like a white witch around the bed. "Does she look pregnant?"

I pointed a little northward at the bitten breast. "Her breasts do."

I opened a zippered pouch on my clamshell while Denholm gave me the preliminaries. "The birthmark is caused by abnormal distribution of blood vessels."

"Thank you," I said.

"The hyoid bone in her neck has been broken."

I turned to Tia. "She's been strangled." I paused. "Do you know anything about her sex life?"

Tia sneered. "It isn't autoerotic, and she didn't ask her boyfriend to do it. She's celibate anyway, for spiritual and health reasons."

"Then we're looking at a murder attempt," I said. It would be a full-blown murder beef if we kept letting her languish here and her fever got worse. If she said she'd activate her hemlock mod if brought to the hospital, then being brought to her employer's house was probably the best option. The Die Off Society had won their suit with the Schengen Government. They'd triumphed on Malthusian, pragmatic grounds relating to carbon footprints rather than the moral justification they'd sought, but they'd won nonetheless. They now had the right to kill themselves, even in hospital or hospice.

I'd found what I was looking for in my jacket. Tia glanced at the needle with widening eyes. "What are you getting ready to shoot her full of?"

"Nothing," I said, "though I may take a sample for later review." It was serendipitous that my client had taken me to the Chinese Node, since my forensic contact Lazlo was in this neighborhood anyway. I was modded out, but certain things were too weird or complicated for me to unriddle on my own. Having a second set of eyes on a sample never hurt.

"Transmitting voice sample." The pained moans that Kyra emitted traveled from me to Denholm.

"Received," the Englishman said.

"Denholm, search the body for latent prints, especially around the wounded neck area."

"Searching, sir."

I clutched the barrel of the hypo in my left hand. Ms. Mifune's eyes remained locked on the needle, as if she didn't trust me not to mercy overdose her employee.

"This is odd, sir," Denholm said, a short time later.

"What?"

Our conversation was two-way encrypted. Even if Tia was tuned into her own subvoc mod, she wouldn't have heard us without top shelf spoofing software. "I get a positive sir, but when I attempt to read the prints for comparison against Central, I also get a message."

I held up a hand, as if Denholm were in front of me and could see the gesture rather than being a disembodied voice in my head broadcasting from a remote location. "Wait, wait. Don't tell me. Something about a digital watermark failing to be authenticated?"

"Correct, sir. Would you like to hear the whole message?"

"Save it," I said. I meant that in the sense of "spare me," but he was a literal-minded bot and would store the info for later. I lifted one of Kyra's cold hands toward me. I could feel the life leaving her body through her fingertips. I glanced at the whorls of her prints and sent the info back to Denholm.

"Switch from latent to personal prints."

"Working, sir."

"I can wait."

The light from the red lantern above the bed caught a glowing, bluish trickle trailing from the bite marks in the engorged breast. How could Kyra be lactating and not pregnant? I looked to Tia. I figured she might slap me, but I had a favor to ask. "We have to unravel this pregnant, not pregnant quandary."

"It is weird," she allowed.

"How close with her were you?"

The nostrils flared again and the black eyes watered. "She's not dead yet, Mr. Moglich."

"How close with her *are* you?" I didn't want to waste the afternoon on semantics.

"Very," she spit the syllable out as if she had been asked to gargle with a mouthful of acid.

"Do you know if she was menstruating, or if she talked about having problems with her cycle?"

My sixth sense tingled, and I waited for a slap from one of those two delicate hands. "Perhaps I should qualify my statement," she seethed so that her tongue peeked momentarily between her lips, like that of an asp. Her gesture left a light coat of gloss on her lips. "We were close enough to talk about more than the weather, but we didn't talk about every bowel movement."

No matter. My forensic contact would be good enough to clarify the pregnancy ambiguity without the kind of teeth pulling I was going through with Ms. Mifune. Denholm saved me further humiliation by breaking in on the subvoc line. His report was ready, or at least his attempt was complete. "Sir, this is equally strange."

"Don't tell me. Required authentication failed due to some more watermark horseshit."

"Equestrian feces don't enter into the equation sir."

"They always do."

He didn't understand that, so he went on with his report as instructed. "Ms. Kyra Boxer had a fingerprint graft job. Those are not her original fingerprints. She has undergone a full identity change."

I looked to Tia, held up the clammy hand of the unfortunate woman on the bed. "She had a print swipe. Did she ever tell you anything about that?"

Tia didn't look surprised, so I suspected she knew. "She said she owed a big student loan debt, about fifty large in dark coin or five in credits. She said it was cheaper to pay for the graft and start over with the skills she picked up in school."

"A lot of kids try that and get caught." I knew it was called pulling a snowbird, though I didn't claim to understand the etymology even if I could understand the logic behind dodging the creditors. Who the hell wanted to pay their debt?

"Okay," I said. That explained that, though it didn't give us a suspect. I doubted that angry creditors who managed to track her down would strangle her and bite her breast. "Let's get to the bite mark."

I leaned down at the bedside. "Let's," Tia said. I had the feeling that I had upset her with my callousness, but I was certain she didn't doubt my skill or competency. Whatever goodwill I'd accrued after rescuing her from rape had probably been squandered, though.

"Denholm?"

"Sir?"

"Tell me what you noticed about the breasts, specifically the right one. Pay especial attention to the bite."

"Yes sir, there is an abscess where the bite took place. It appears to be leading quickly to a painful infection. If not treated, it can lead to death."

"Denholm, I want you to establish a link with Tia Mifune after we conclude business here and I head to Lazlo's lab for sample analysis. I need you to tell her everything you've told me, do you understand?"

"Yes sir."

"Good." I didn't have time to keep Ms. Mifune apprised of every detail on my way to solving this case, so Denholm's assistance would help keep her in the loop. I probed the breast tissue in a clinical manner, around the red wound. I pointed to the bloody lump. "What is this red wound?"

"Sir, it is a benign cyst that contains milk."

I turned to Tia. "She is lactating." I subvoc'd again with Denholm. "And what's causing this cyst?"

"It is usually caused by blockage of a milk duct, though it usually doesn't become infected. Exact diagnosis would require either ultrasound or needle aspiration."

"I left my ultrasound machine at home," I said, sarcastically, "but I've got a needle."

"Careful," Tia said, her tone softer now.

"I will be. Denholm," I subvoc'd, "is there a chance this thing could explode if I pierce it with my needle?"

"I don't think so, sir."

"Alright, then. I'm going to try to get a visual impression of the bite mark. I need you to construct a three-dimensional model on that, and then compare that to all dental records with Central. Do you understand?"

"It will take some time, but I will have the model shaped and compared."

I stared at the bite mark. "Making dental impression." It looked like whoever had bit Kyra boxer's breast had a healthy set of thirty-two adult choppers. It was always possible that there was some gap or irregularity that could narrow the field down, or that some evidence of shoddy bridgework or a crown made of a material used only by certain companies or corporations could be found. The prevailing wisdom was usually that the worse the teeth, the more likely the case could be solved with dental impressions. I doubted we were going to crack this case with a bite mark, but nothing ventured meant nothing gained.

"Impression received," Denholm said, "Three-dimensional model being constructed."

"Outstanding work, Denny."

"Thank you sir."

"If you get something good, send your findings to Forensic Dentistry Inc. and have them make a plaster cast. Pay with dark coin."

"Yes sir."

"End session, Denholm. Go speedily to thy work."

"Yes, sir."

I wasted no more time with the needle and sunk the bevel into the sore breast tissue leaking milk. I spoke to Tia as I pulled the plunger back and the barrel of the hypo filled with an admixture of bluish breast milk and swirling trails of red blood. "Whoever bit your friend also is probably mixed up in the Blankstone murder." The needle was full and I capped the bevel, which dripped a single teardrop-shaped speck of blood.

"What makes you say that?"

"Whoever bombed Schengen Palace covered their tracks with the same wipe encryption as whoever bit and strangled your girl."

"So you're sure she was strangled?"

"That's what my sources tell me. The damage is internal, no ligatures or bruises on the neck."

"I'm starting to get scared." I wondered if she meant she feared losing her business or her life, or both. She was involved in something that included some pretty heavy hitters, some powerbrokers and killers, whether she wanted to be involved or not. Ditto for me.

"Do your employees carry recording mods?"

"Yes, but confidentiality agreements mean they can't be recording while in session with a client. It would be a violation of trust."

"I don't want to insinuate Kyra would violate a patient's trust-"

"Client," Tia said, "not patient."

"Client," I checked myself. "But maybe she accidentally left it on during a session or something. If so, we might be able to get a good look at the face of the shit bag who bit and strangled her."

"It's possible," Tia said.

What I didn't say was that a theory was already forming in my mind that might cast her employee and friend in a less than stellar light. It was only a half-formed theory, but I thought it was possible that Kyra and maybe some other employees were using their recording features while with clients despite contractual stipulations to the contrary. The touch may have been considered "platonic," but then again maybe she thought she could use the sessions as evidence of infidelity. She had maybe tried the ploy with someone whose hardware was good enough for him to know she was lying about not recording, and he had bitten and strangled her in retaliation for the betrayal of trust and attempt at extortion.

It was a possibility.

"What now?" Tia asked.

I placed the stoppered hypo into one of the zippered pouches on the clamshell. "Now I get this sample tested." I pointed to the pocket where the needle full of blood and milk was secured. "Then we go from there."

"Thank you," Tia bowed slightly.

"Thank you," I said, walking toward the front door. She walked with me, and we left the poor fevered woman to suffer and writhe on the bed in her delirium. Tia opened the front door and I stepped out into the hallway. I stood on the door's threshold and spoke quietly, just in case some busybody was watching us through a keyhole.

"I'm praying for your friend to pull through. If she doesn't, make sure the computer forensic pathologists check all her mods for journals, recordings, and any private log of activity she may have kept that might give us a window into whatever was going on with her."

"Will do," Tia said, and closed the door on me. My hands were still wet from the sweat of Kyra Boxer's hand. I ran the slicked palm through my hair that had turned white from terror a long time ago.

CHAPTER SIX

LAZLO'S CURIOSITIES

My contact's shop was located between Madame Vang's massage parlor and Lau's East-West Import Export. The massage parlor's storefront was obscured except for the neon by the cooking grease emanating from a neighboring Chinese restaurant. Trussed Peking ducks hung upside down and skinless in the window. Lau's was such a shade tree operation that it didn't even have a front entrance. Rumor had it Madame Vang's trafficked in smuggled human cargo from the Edge, luring refugees into either sex worker or domestic indentured servitude. The import-export operation with the bricked-up windows was said to be a front for a gun and drug-running operation.

There was no substance to the rumors about what went on in the massage parlor, but it was an open secret that SPD closed an eye and took a bribe from Lau Ng now and again. He at least kept a lid on the chaos that might have erupted between triads that would have otherwise been involved in constant block-to-block gunfights without the iron hand of a local strongman.

I wondered what Miss Mifune would have said about the massage parlor's holistic merits as I opened the door to Lazlo's Curiosities. Everything in the shop came to life at once, startling me to the point where I almost reacted like a bull in a china shop. I looked around. Most stores had door chimes to let the indisposed staff in the back of the shop know there were customers up front. Lazlo had a whole damn menagerie, an army of toys.

A miniature violinist made of tortured and sculpted biscuit tin agitated the catgut on his violin as a Titanic made from upcycled camshafts began to sink. The tortured Heifetz whining that seemed to come from the violinist really came from a gramophone hidden somewhere else in the shop, but I knew that only because Lazlo showed it to me on one of my previous visits.

"Just a minute!" He shouted from the back of the store.

"Take your time." I reflexively felt for the hypo that was filled with its strange brew, secured in my jacket.

I looked around the room, which was as cluttered as an old wives' apothecary. There were wood kits for amateur hobbyists lining the walls. Crank-operated hand-painted jacks waited in their boxes for some unsuspecting hand to turn their gears and spring clowns from hiding. Birds made of tinplate were nesting in the Bavarian wood of cuckoo clocks that had similar designs, although they sprung free from hiding on the hour every hour. I checked my internal clock and realized I had just missed this hour's chiming. I felt as disappointed as a child who showed up at the circus just as the big top was packing it in.

Lazlo stuck his head out from the back of the shop, splitting the gypsy bead curtain divider. "Oh, it's you. Come on back."

"I catch you at a bad time?"

I walked forward, toward his voice. "I'm always busy, if that's what you mean."

A motion-sensor activated diorama was triggered at my approach. I thanked God Lazlo put his skills to such innocence ends, at least when I was crossing his path. Penguins gathered around an egg made of shaped white Milliput, on spruce painted to resemble an ice floe. A hatchling sprung from the cracked egg, and revealed itself to be a chicken. I laughed at the bit of transgenic cuckoldry, although the ceramic penguin figurines didn't look quite so amused.

"Hope you're decent." I split the bead curtain with my hands clasped together, and turned left.

Lazlo was seated in front of his workbench. A power jigsaw, its teeth filled with fine wood, lay next to a set of engineer's pliers and a spirit level. My friend turned toward me, wearing his trademark black aviator goggles. I had never seen him without them and I wondered what color his eyes were. I had heard from others that his eyes were milky as cataracts due to botched eye implants. He wore a Samedi grey felt top hat and the tips of his Dali moustache were stiff with model glue he used in place of wax to give the whiskers their especial hold.

"What brings you here?"

I opened a zippered pouch on my clamshell and handed him the hypo. I had no idea what was going on with his eyes, but his lips pursed. "What have we here?"

I shrugged. "I was hoping you would tell me that."

"That can be done."

I didn't feel like haggling. I was all credited up after running across Tia Mifune, besides which my curiosity was piqued. Lazlo reached for his own wand on the table before him. His sticker was disguised as a Swiss Army Knife, and he held the little red instrument out toward mine while stating his terms. "Fifty in credits."

It wasn't a question, and I knew I couldn't talk him down. It wasn't greed that motivated him either, but a desire to keep playing with his toys. I conceded, clicked my sticker, and nodded. I glanced around the room. "It takes that much juice to run this place?"

Lazlo stood quickly and I wondered how his top hat always stayed on his head. I'd forgotten how tall he was, gaunt as an undertaker and thin as a hunger artist in his cage. "I need the credits for alloys, recycled metal, not light or water."

I squinted. "Since when does metal count as energy?"

"Since I learned to spoof the converter, so I could trade credits for something more substantial." I didn't want to pry into his black marketeering. I watched him as he walked over to his forensics setup and squirted a bit of the milk onto the glass plate. "How long have you had this?"

"About an hour," I said.

"It's got some sort of coolant adulterating it then." He touched the rest of the solution remaining in the chamber of the hypo. "This should be room temperature by now or getting there, and it isn't."

He studied the petri dish with his black bug eyes, and then carried it over to another part of the shop. "Wait here."

I did as I was told. I turned around, triggering another whirligig behind me. Carnival music started up, counterpointed by Lazlo's boast. "Feel free to have a look at that. A little something new I'm working on."

I leaned down to the three-ringed circus he'd fashioned. "Now I see why you need the credits."

"Idle hands ..."

A ballerina with exposed breasts bounded upward onto a trapeze, cinching the wires in her kung-fu grip. A more gravitationally handicapped strongman looked up with what I thought was envy in his tiny eyes, jealous

45

that he couldn't fly like the lithe woman in the white leotard. Some sort of unseen camshaft mechanism caused the strongman to lift his weighted barbell in time with a sword swallower's devouring of a double-edged blade in his wide maw. Both men wore striped, one piece old-timey midway swimsuits.

"I'm back," Lazlo said.

"Hey," I said, remembering something.

"What?"

"You've heard about the bombing at Schengen Palace?"

His shoulders shrugged. He seemed annoyed. "Who hasn't?"

"You know anything about this 'digital watermark not authenticated' spoof?"

His Cheshire grin was so wide that for a moment I thought he might be behind the program. I chucked the idea in the next instant. Lazlo was a tinker and tinkerer, not a sadist. He could admire and deconstruct the most cutting edge software, but his heart was in antiques and ephemera.

"I've tried breaking that code," he said. "Whoever did that knows their shit, even better than I know mine."

"And you know your shit."

"I know." He stepped aside, revealing a clockwork duck made of gilt brass. "I brought a friend." He patted the duck on its bill.

"What the hell is that?"

"I told you," he said, "It's my friend."

The thing waddled from foot-to-foot, like a windup toy. Its stomach was clear, like a visible man model. Flexible rubber tubing was coiled in the stomach and wound on itself like a strand of long intestine. Closer scrutiny revealed that some of the white fluid from the syringe was circulating through the bird's belly.

Lazlo held up the syringe with the remainder of the milk still inside. "I've got enough of a sample for Ducky to tell me a thing or two. Do you mind if I hang onto this to run some more tests?"

"No," I said, shaking my head. "The longer you have it, the more you can probably learn. All I ask is that you tell me what you find out."

"Will do." Lazlo walked the hypo back over to his workbench and set it down next to his tools. He pointed at the duck's stomach where the milk flowed. "Where'd you get this stuff, anyway?"

"I'm on a case," I said, growing pensive.

"I understand. Client-dick confidentiality."

"You've got it."

He stroked the toy duck's silky pelt, as if it was a real pet. I wondered how lonely he was, and thought he probably could have used some TLC from Touch LLC. I caught myself mid-judgment, and remembered that a butler bot was my own best friend.

"You still at the Zhakpot?"

I nodded. Lazlo licked his lips. "Yeah, I'd like to get myself some of those one-armed bandits. I love the sound those old slot machines make. *Cha-ching!*" His hollered onomatopoeia seemed to be just what the doctor ordered, as Ducky responded to the sound by hotfooting in place with its webbed toes before loosing a watery fart. The duck emitted an Oxo-cube sized bit of fecal matter from the length of prolapsed rubber hose sticking out of its rear.

Lazlo had catlike reflexes and he caught the strange shit before it could hit the floor of his workshop. "Tell me something, Ducky."

The duck turned to Lazlo and spoke in a watery lisp that I recognized as belonging to a twentieth-century cartoon duck. "The sample includes a combination of high protein fore milk produced by the human female at the start of a breastfeeding session, and the high-fat milk produced at the end. The latter is known as hind milk."

Lazlo winked at me. "Learn something new every day."

The duck continued with its analysis. "A parasite similar to Gorgoderid was found in the culture."

"Alive or dead?" Lazlo interrupted Ducky.

"Dying," the duck said. "Residue analysis informs me that the parasite was living in macrophages of female breast tissue, but began to senesce once removed from its host medium."

"What else?"

"The Gorgoderid was mixing *Papivar Bracteatum* with P. Somniferum, to hybridize and produce morphine."

Lazlo's jaw dropped, and I saw he had vampire fang mods for the first time. "That's impossible," he said.

"What is?" I asked.

"All of it." He stood to pace, as if he might be able to walk off his disbelief. "Gorgoderid is a parasite, not a nano-sized drug synthesizer." He lowered his voice, and pointed toward the import-export warehouse to our right. He spoke in a low reverential tone of the kingpin in whose shadow he labored. "I've been working on creating new synths for Lau's crew for a while now, and I never got close to doing what someone programmed this parasite to do."

My eyebrow arched. "Programmed a parasite? I didn't know that was possible."

Lazlo threw up his hands, ego bruised by the superiority of our unseen and now mutual foe. "Neither did I." He stared at me with such intensity that I felt his eyes probing my brainstem, dark goggles or no. "Where did you say you got this sample?"

"From a woman's breast," I said. I had an obligation to keep as much info to myself as possible in order to respect my client, but that had to be balanced against the fact that I knew I was fucked without Lazlo's help.

"That milk would kill a baby," Lazlo said. He was now as confused as I was.

I locked my fingers together and thought of a question. "What would it do to a man?"

Lazlo giggled, showing the fangs again. "It would get him higher than giraffe vagina is what it would do. He'd see dragons on the ceiling for quite a while." He picked up the defecated pellet and hefted it in his palm like a dice he was worried might be loaded in favor of the house. "I might be tempted to suck on that tit, if it didn't have that damn parasite in it."

"The woman whose breast this came from," I said, "she wasn't pregnant. I don't think she was at least, and I don't think she'd given birth recently."

"What makes you say that?"

"She had washboard abs, and I don't think it was a sculpt job. Her friend says she was celibate and I believe her. I don't think she was inseminated, either."

Lazlo set the Oxo cube on the table. "That leaves only one alternative then." He stood, picked his duck up like an infant, and carried it back toward the rear of his workshop. "She was modded out with some kind of mammary implant to give breastmilk laced with a strong, new morphine strain."

I scratched my stubble. "With a little parasite chaser."

"It's possible whoever was sucking her tits didn't know what all they were drinking." He pointed toward his array of equipment behind him. "If I may paraphrase Archimedes, give me a microscope and I'll move the world. My duck barely caught the thing, and for all I know the Gorgon parasite has its own cloaking program that only failed because it was dying and couldn't defend itself anymore."

"You're one step ahead of me," I said, my head spinning.

"I'm one step ahead of everyone," Lazlo said, "except whoever built that parasite."

"Is it organic or a machine?"

"Both," Lazlo said. "Neither." He huffed, exasperated. "Shit, I don't know." This was the first time I'd seen him genuinely stymied. I hated to add another curveball, but it couldn't be helped.

"I think whoever put that parasite in her breast and whoever installed that milk mammary mod also put the hit out on Blankstone."

Lazlo's forehead was a mass of wrinkled putty, a confused crease of flesh as malleable as his clay men. "What makes you say that?"

"She had latent prints on her, but when I tried a lift I got that same stupid digital watermark message encryption."

"This guy knows how to cover his ass."

"Do you think we can catch him?"

Lazlo nodded toward the hypo, stoppered and filled with the bluish milk. "Give me some time with this sample."

"Do you know anyone who does these kinds of mammary mods?"

He laughed at the alliteration. I thought it was ridiculous up to a point. I was also somewhat creeped out, curious, and even sympathetic. If Blankstone had been suckling at Kyra Boxer's breast, who was I to judge him? If a woman came to a man whose days consisted of unending stress and Machiavellian power machinations and she said, in essence, *drink soothing opium from my nipple*, why wouldn't he be tempted to oblige?

"How is she?" Lazlo asked, bringing me out of my thoughts.

"Who?"

"The girl." He pointed toward the hypo.

I stood. "I think she's dying." I turned, and parted the gypsy bead curtain. My own words made me move now with a sense of urgency. "I've got to get going. Let me know what you find."

"I will," Lazlo said, "if you agree to do the same."

"It's a deal."

He took the needle in his hands and twirled it, admiring the crystal body of the hypo barrel. I wondered if he was maybe crazy enough to inject it into his own veins. "I hope they catch this bastard, and cast his ass into the Edge. But I want to meet him before they exile him. I'd like to compliment him on his craftsmanship" Lazlo flashed the vampire fangs one last time. "I've never met someone smarter than me."

CHAPTER SEVEN

KYRA'S HOUSE

Touching base with Tia Mifune via subvoc revealed that Kyra Boxer was still alive and that she resided in a studio apartment nestled among the super-blocks of the Green Node. The CEO of Touch LLC informed me that her wounded client still refused to go to the hospital, and that hourly re-dressing of the wound over her breast kept inflammation from getting out of control.

A twenty-minute ride on the snake from the Casino Node put me in Kyra's neighborhood. Things were still damp from the last cloud seeding, and rain barrels on roofs carpeted with seasonal grasses were overflowing. Everything had a dull blue-grey tint to it in the wake of the fog. Bioluminescents were outlawed in this Node, which muddied the colors of everything further. Bicyclists in neon form-fitting outfits peddled for all their calf implants were worth. Residents confident the rain had ended for now were out tending to their front yard vegetable patches. I admired the ethics of the people who lived here, and I didn't mind visiting. After a while though, vat-grown protein didn't taste like beef no matter how carefully it was cultivated.

Kyra's building was sandwiched between two steel-alloy bike racks half-filled with lightweight chrome jobs. The place was only three stories tall. It was seated on the foundation of what was previously part of the maglev rail bed whose arteries had been diverted in another direction to green up in this part of town.

I looked at the platinum-covered house ID unit out-front. It was voice-op. "Denholm?"

"Yes sir?"

"Verify the voice sample on file for Kyra Boxer."

I heard the pained moan of the woman coming into my ear. "This one, sir?"

"Yes, patch it through."

"Done, sir."

I spoke to the box in front of the building. "Please let me in."

"Ms. Boxer!" The box spoke like a gravel-voiced man. I wondered why she had selected that custom. "Welcome home."

The front door opened. Inside the walls of the entryway were made of white swirling stuccos. An Edge migrant ran a feather duster across the bannister and ignored my approach. I climbed the creaking wooden stairs to the third floor. Kyra's door was the only one in the hallway. Soft grey carpet masked my footfalls. I looked at the wainscoted doorframe. A small box lodged in the center of the door revealed the security to be another voice-box job.

"I'm home."

"Ms. Boxer, please state your password."

"Denholm?"

"Sir?" The dry English accent was in my ear. "Try now, sir."

I got a little shock at how heuristic he was, doing my will without my having to ask or do more than state his name. "Password accepted," the door said. I gripped the knob and walked inside.

A floor cooling unit activated the moment I stepped into the studio apartment. The breeze was strong enough to untuck bloused pant legs. I shivered and walked forward. I was in the kitchen. The floor was covered in ruby art deco tiles. The honeycombed pattern repeated throughout the studio, giving it the impression of a giant bathroom or natatorium.

"Well, this should be easy," I said. "It's just one room."

"Sir?"

"Go to sleep," I said, and Denholm was gone from my sub-vocalization mod. I scanned with my eyes before going forward. I had my druthers gun-wise in the Casino Node, but the power of the Greens here meant that if I was caught packing I could get a five-year exile. I might be able to spoof my way back in somehow, but if caught my banishment would be compounded by a fine that would have eaten my down payment on this job from Ms. Mifune.

I bunched my fist and prepared to throw the cybered left if it came to that. I heard a loud noise from my right, and what sounded like the crack of a rifle report. I hit the deck hard enough to bruise my elbows. I laughed when I saw what had caused the sound.

The door of the dishwasher was open, and steam hissed out as the appliance spoke to me. "Ms. Boxer, your cycle is done."

I waited for the steam to waft away and spoke in what the appliance thought was the voice of its owner. "It's been awhile since I've been home."

"I know, Ms. Boxer."

"I forget, what was the cycle program I ran?"

I stood back up from the tile, massaging my sore elbows. "Ms. Boxer, you requested a sterilization cycle. I made sure to maintain a constant temperature of one-hundred degrees Fahrenheit. You have been charged one-eighth of a credit."

"That's pretty steep."

"I am sorry. I do not understand."

"That is an excessive charge."

"You did not program me to stop cycling," the machine said. I thought it odd that something inanimate could adopt what I thought was a defensive tone. "Most of the washing was done by reclaimed night water."

"That puts my mind at ease." I walked forward and pulled out the racks of the dishwasher. They dripped with sopping water. The bottom rack was empty. The top was filled with plastic flanges and seashells.

"I sustained an injury while riding a bicycle," I said.

"I am sorry to hear that, Ms. Boxer. I was also not aware that you owned a bicycle."

I had taken a chance with that comment. I figured it was a dollars to donuts proposition that one of the jobs on the rack below was hers. "A lot has changed since we last spoke."

"Yes, ma'am."

The ball was in my court. I didn't want to provoke any kind of built-in identity theft alert I might trigger with suspicious questions or statements, so I treaded carefully. "I sustained a concussion while riding my bike."

"I am sorry to hear that, Ms. Boxer. I should say though that a quick scan reveals that you did not go to the hospital."

"I'm averse to them, as you may know."

"I am aware of a hemlock mod and a standing DNR clause on your file."

"Still, my head hurts and I cannot for the life of me remember what exactly I was washing in here. I can't even remember if I named you."

The machine seemed to buy all of what I was selling. "You named me

'The Best Boyfriend in the World,' because you said I was the only man you knew who would do dishes."

"I see."

"I will be happy to describe the contents of the top rack to you, Ms. Boxer. There are no items currently in the bottom rack."

I reached into the top rack and picked up a light seashell, one of five in the rack. I held it in my palm. "Why was I washing seashells?"

"Ms. Boxer, you said that sometimes your nipples were sore and that the seashells were the second-best method for keeping your breasts cool."

"What was the best method?"

"Cabbage leaves that had been left in the freezer," the dishwasher said.

"I can't remember why I didn't use cabbage leaves, then."

"Ms. Boxer, you claimed that 'the bitch next door' stole your cabbages from the garden patch."

"I see. You mentioned the freezer?"

"Yes ma'am."

"I forget where it is."

A coffin panel on the wall opened and a white Freon-free Ice Max appeared. "Thank you Best Boyfriend in the World. You may sleep." I turned to the freezer and spoke to it. "Hello."

"Welcome back, Ms. Boxer. Fred has missed you." The male voice had an uncanny resemblance to the one chosen for the voice-box. I wondered if Fred might not have been the name of one of her non-dishwashing real boyfriends whose lackluster performance in the sack or infidelity had caused Kyra to turn her household appliances into a surrogate male support system.

"Has anyone been here since I've been gone?"

"Yes."

My heart jumped in my chest. "Who?"

"Digital watermark authentication failed. No file found."

Motherfucker. I should have known that whoever was playing cat and mouse with me could have come through here and done what I was now doing. Their skillset was obviously larger than mine, so why couldn't they also spoof everything to think they were Kyra Boxer? I was starting to think the 'digital watermark' hack was a deliberate way for whoever knew I was on their trail to fuck with my head. If that was the case, it was working.

I opened the freezer door and got hit with an arctic blast. Frostbitten protein-based meat simulation and soy ice cream shrouded in gusts of cold air surrounded an igloo built of ice blocks. I pulled one block free and the whole house of cards came tumbling down. Inside of the miniature Eskimo abode were several bottles of frozen milk. I figured that whatever was in the bottles was also in the sample I'd given to Lazlo, and he already had his hands full.

"Fred, I need to hit the co-op today for groceries. I want to plan a party. What does your memory say about my friends' preferences when they come over?"

"Viva prefers the soy mocha ice cream."

"Viva?"

"That is the only name she has provided."

"What about my other friends?"

"Ms. Boxer, you have specifically stated that Viva's voice signature is the only one other than your own whose authentication I am to accept."

"I guess all of my appliances have the same directive."

"They do."

"Okay." I hated to wake Denholm, since I thought he needed cooldown time and maybe some routine maintenance. It looked like I needed him again, though. "Wake up."

"Good afternoon, sir."

I didn't have time for the pleasantries. "Run a fingerprint scan on all items in the freezer, especially on those touching this." I focused my eyes on a pyramid of ice cream, staring down the half-eaten pint of soy mocha. "Skip the graft jobs you find. We already established the modded prints belong to Kyra. Also, skip the ones that won't authenticate. Give me a third set, if you can."

"I can, sir."

My heartbeat sped up. "Shoot."

"Partial, left hand, Viva Jasmine."

"Wonderful!" I could get a full breakdown later, but I decided to do a prelim before walking into the living room. I closed the fridge door and said, "Run her against Central."

I walked into the main living space. The walls were bare, except for a couple of impressionistic watercolors framed in ornate gold-gilt. The frames probably cost more than the two reproductions, one of a nude woman supine on an ottoman and the other a vase of yellow flowers next to a bowl of fruit.

"Jasmine, Viva. Alias Jasmine, Diva. Three tattoos, fifteen-percent modded, one prior arrest, one report to Central Collections."

Something strange in the right corner of the room caught my eye. It appeared to be an oversized crib. Its nautilus-shaped shell was made of black canvas, as if it might be designed to rock an undead baby and soothe its blood-filled stomach whenever the sun went down and the moon was full.

My heart was racing so fast I couldn't do anything besides whisper my query to Denholm. "What are the mods?" I asked. I walked carefully toward the crib. If I'd had a gun, I would have pulled it. I wasn't sure what I was expecting to find in the crib, maybe a gorgon-like parasite in the guise of an infant.

"One bio-lumo tattoo above the left breast, a 'Viva' tattoo whose first letter can shift to 'D' based on heart rhythms."

"Clever," I said. It probably segued from "Viva" to "Diva" when an orgasm was imminent. "What about the other ones? A tattoo does not a fifteen percent mod make."

"The other ones are confidential, as they are covered under the Right to Privacy Act unless a warrant for inquiry is made and approved."

"Never mind." I would find her and ask her myself, if and when I made it out of here alive. That black crib was calling my name. I walked around toward the front of it. I was greeted by a decapitated baby head mounted on the red clay body of an Egyptian god doll fetish of some kind.

"What the fuck? Denholm, help me before I lose my mind."

"Mama…" The baby whined, and its mouth puckered. I stowed the reflexive urge to swing and shatter its glass jaw and muffle its creepy mewling that made my skin crawl. The rubbery lips puckered to suckle. I regretted spoofing the appliances to think I was her. There was no way I was going to feed this thing.

"Sir, the unit currently speaking belongs to a hospital-grade medical breast pump. Its cycles-per-minute and suction strength have both been designed to mimic the action of a real infant feeding."

"Okay." I was relieved to see that it was a robot and we weren't dealing with a literal baby, but other than that I was still scared shitless. "What's up with the body?"

"Sir, I've located an explanation in your general education mod."

"Thank you." I cursed myself for being too lazy to check for myself. I was getting spoiled having Denholm around. I made a mental note to try some cursive when I got home to keep my mind and my mods from turning to mush.

"The body belongs to a replica of an ancient statue of the bird-headed Egyptian Goth Thoth."

"That explains that," I said. It didn't however explain why she created this hybrid god-baby for suckling. I thought about the little I knew about the woman's breastmilk, based on my initial contact with Lazlo. I spoke to my mod directly now, rather than using Denholm as a conduit. "Check Gods, Egyptian, Thoth. Check all works relating to the aforementioned and drugs of any kind."

"Done." It had taken the mod three tenths of a second to peruse every written document, every recorded PhD seminar, every archeologist's observation scribbled at an excavation site that was later scanned and uploaded to Central for posterity.

"Random sample," I said.

The general education mod started talking in my head. I had my ER unit turned off, since I needed my eyes to do more than read right now. "The Greek physician Galen was a firm believer in the medical curative properties of opium, which was rumored to have been brought to mankind by the bird-headed Egyptian god Thoth."

That explained something. I was about to bring Denholm back into the fray, and request that he use my contact lens stored over his eye to do a subdural readout on the baby-god mutant. I spotted a compartment on the front of the little doll that resembled an oversized battery pouch, which made the need for Denholm's x-ray intercession unnecessary. This was assuming I could open the compartment.

I pulled it free, and cursed myself for not getting Denholm to do a scan anyway before I went ahead and opened it. I was so eager to satisfy my curiosity that I hadn't bothered to consider that whoever was playing games with me was playing deadly games, and that he might have booby-trapped the bird baby.

It was too late to turn back. I withdrew my hand in disgust as the baby with parched lips tried to suckle one of my knuckles after it lightly touched his mouth. Inside of the body of the Thoth doll was a half-filled bottle of milk that I suspected had been expressed from Kyra Boxer's breast. I figured the solution was the same as that in the freezer, or that which leaked from her breast. I thought about picking up the device and bringing it to Lazlo, who as a tinker and toymaker might find it perversely fascinating. I discarded the idea in the next moment. I couldn't stare at that creepy baby for another moment. I definitely couldn't pick it up in my arms and cradle it over to Lazlo's Wonder Chamber in Chinatown. I had another solid lead anyway. I was done playing with toys for now.

I stepped back and spoke to Denholm. "Place this crib for me, would you?"

"Searching…" I turned around the room, and walked toward the far wall. Another feature of the house startled to life, as one fourth of the room lifted like a postmodern portcullis and revealed a balcony. I was beyond being surprised, and I walked forward onto the balcony.

My butler bot's voice came to me. "The model is a Tincture of Time. It is made to rock infants to sleep. It comes with Handel's Water Music stock, made to play through unidirectional speakers. It can rock at ten different speeds and retails for-"

"That's a pretty big crib," I said. Denholm never got offended when I interrupted him.

"Yes sir. The model you broadcast to me apparently has a berth that has been modified."

"To fit a man."

"It could feasibly accommodate most grown men. Yes, sir."

"Thank you Denholm. Have room service bring up a steak with ten percent meat, well-done, a wedge of bleu cheese, and a mineral cola." I didn't want the Green Node's veganism or health consciousness rubbing off on me too much.

"Yes sir."

I ran my fingers through my white hair, whispered "Shit" under my breath, and exhaled mightily. I walked to the edge of the balcony. I always had a bit of vertigo, but there was no risk of falling since the edge of the balcony ended where a photovoltaic wall disguised as glass skin began. The panels were so close that after I exhaled, the tinted plate nearest me fogged over from the force of my breath. I wiped the smudged pane and glanced out in the direction of Heat Island.

The energy collection points were scattered on a series of archipelagos in a linked chain, separated one from the other by freshwaters. The silos and cisterns were arrayed in an ever-repeating pattern from one island to the next, interspersed with onyx-skinned solar panel clusters lined up like furrows in a field that fed machines instead of men. There was nothing especially sinister about Heat Island, but from this vantage it looked like a top-secret weapons facility. I occasionally got feeds from aerial drones when my enhanced reality mod was active, and from the sky the archipelagos looked like a series of circuit boards arranged in the gridded network that was the greater Schengen City computer. It was a living hive, half-organic and half-synthetic like that parasite swimming through the milk.

I turned from the balcony. Enough sightseeing.

CHAPTER EIGHT

VANILLA TOMORROW NIGHT

My Enhanced Reality mod showed me that Viva Jasmine had been arrested for prostitution once in my neck of the woods, and that a charge for possession of a yeast capable of reproducing opiates had been expunged from her formal record. A quick ping brought the announcement from Jasmine to all her social dendrites and lurkers that she would be at a Kink and Synth fete hosted in the Kunstler Civic Plaza tonight. I was already in the Green Node, so I decided to hang back. I'd get lunch, enjoy breathable air, and partake of walkable trails for a few hours.

When I was done walking I sat at an outdoor café. Stickley furniture was arranged around tables aimed toward an eco-village done in Tudorbethan style. I could live here I thought, or at least retire here. The idea of dying of old age in a casino resort was not all that appealing to me. By the time late afternoon segued to dusk, I was still sipping coffee. The barista started giving me dirty looks, so I took the cue. I left a tip, got up, and went for another walk.

The moon eventually rose, splitting through the diamond lattice covering the gazebo in the park where I walked. Couples pushing strollers and flying kites gave way to night traffic, mostly kids wearing biolumo bracelets and swinging glow sticks. They were flaunting an ordinance by wearing the radiant but environmentally poisonous toys.

I found the brick building where my quarry announced she would be for the night. It was next to a stone water feature of a crane perched on one leg. I didn't know Viva Jasmine from Eve, and I thought it was more than possible that she was a flake who might say she was going to be somewhere and then not show up.

The snaking queue I joined was thick with revelers in fetish wear. They were dressed in leather or chiffon undergarments, covered in electroluminescent wires that translated every small movement into a new light effect. The doorman wore a neck pendant that was a pulsing circuit board. He was bald, ruddy, and had golden eagle feather implants jutting from the top of his skull that formed a headdress.

"You look a little out of place," he said, and revealed a mouthful of filed teeth.

"That makes sense, as I'm not here to party."

The bouncer looked around me and waved more fashionistas in. "Yeah well, neither are these people. Tonight things are a bit more serious. Why don't you come back tomorrow for Vanilla Night?"

"What's that?"

The night sky glowed with light refracted from the costumes of those below. "That's the more traditional snuggle party," someone spoke, but he was unseen behind his beefy henchman. A small man with a neckbeard bordering on Amish proportions stepped around the heavy. The big guy showed deference, which I took to mean that this was his boss.

"Russell Nadler," the man said, and took me to the side diplomatically. I shook his right hand.

"Detective John Moglich."

He had a wide natural smile, and didn't seem insecure about his yellow-filmed choppers. He looked like the kind of man who was too preoccupied with some mental project to do much hygiene. I recognized him from the news feeds I sometimes checked in my head or had Denholm project onto the ceiling of my bedroom back in the Zhakpot.

It *was* Russell Nadler. "You're the one who came up with the T-cell replication mod."

"Guilty as charged," he said.

Now I understood where he got the money for his short notice fetes, and why he gave off such a friendly vibe. If my lifework was trying to treat disease and sometimes doing it successfully, I might also forget to brush my teeth every once and awhile.

"What can I help you with?" he asked.

"I need to talk to this woman." I sent him a photo from one of her social dendrites, rather than the mugshot. If I sent him a police file photo, he would assume I was with the police.

He was a little suspicious anyway. "What has she done?"

"Nothing," I said. "She's not in any trouble, not with the law at least. She might have a stalker. A friend has hired me to look out for her and let her know to be on her guard."

I'd made all that up on the fly. Anyone as pretty, young, and socially active as her who'd also dabbled in drugs might plausibly find herself the victim of a stalking campaign. My words might not have even been a lie; for all I knew whoever had bitten Kyra Boxer was also planning on taking a bite out of Viva.

"Follow me," he said, and I did. His gorilla looked disappointed that his chance to bounce me had passed. Maybe he figured that crippling me in front of the crowd might get one of the girls in sado-maso gear moist for him.

"Jimmy was right to try to keep you out," Russell said. I followed him inside of the hangar-sized building, whose inner shell was skinned over in black-lighted PVC tarpaulin. I walked through the glowing throng. It smelled of beer foam and body odor. The floor beneath my feet felt like an inflated tire, sort of like in the Zero G sim moonwalks.

"Yeah, apparently he said tomorrow night would have been more my speed."

A ticket girl with a spiked dog-collar choker and color shifting sleeve tats took money from customers, and pressed a button that let our twosome pass through the turnstile without paying. We were on catwalk scaffolding, elevated above the convention floor.

"My parties are all about touch," Nadler said. A strobe light kicked in. I struggled to see and hear him through the seizure-inducing light and music, which sounded like sheet metal being punctured in four-four time. "On Vanilla Night it's mostly couples looking for a PJ party. They do puppy piles, pillow fights. They cuddle. We also have a night set aside just for involuntarily celibate men to do confidence-building exercises with women." He acknowledged the respectful nod of a partygoer passing us on the catwalk. "Some of them do eye-gazing and synchronized breathing. You know," he said, "you can touch with the eye."

He opened his palm, revealing a grafted third eye lodged there. He closed his own eyes, and the brown eye in the center of the lifelines of his hand searched with its roving gaze. "Hold up any number of fingers on your right hand."

I played his game and shot him rabbit ears. "Two," he said, with the eyes in his head closed. He lowered his palm, and I regretted shaking his hand. He laughed at my unease and waved for me to follow him. "Come on." We descended the steps, passing a woman wearing gladiatrix rubber and leading her naked man-slave by a chain attached to the Prince Albert piercing in his penis. I gave them a wide berth.

"Diva Jasmine is her name, yes?" Russel said, of the image I'd flashed him.

"Yeah," I said. I didn't want to tell him it was actually Viva and blow her cover or whatever kind of character she'd created for herself. I wondered what her exact relationship to Kyra Boxer was, aside from raiding her fridge for mocha ice cream. There was a good chance she was a coworker at Touch LLC. This place was all about sensual touch, at least on vanilla night. I would run it all by Tia Mifune in the near-future, to see what she knew about Viva/Diva Jasmine.

We walked through the crush of sculpted bodies, which ran the gambit from semi-nude to naked. I definitely felt overdressed and out of place. I was grateful to be ferried through the throng now by the treater of AIDS. He was a hero to hedonists and squares alike, scourge though to Big Pharm. I wondered if he was connected to this case in some way, aside from knowing Viva and where she was in all this madness on the floor.

"Did you like this?" He held his palm out to me again, and the eye inside his hand winked.

"I thought I'd seen every mod," I said.

"Dermo-optical relays aren't easy to do. It's just like any other mod. You have to meet criteria to even be an applicant, and then there's no guarantee that yours will take."

"It looks like yours took," I said. He could have just guessed that I had been holding up two fingers, or perhaps he had a more standard internal camera relay that told him I was shooting him the peace sign.

"Mine did take, but do you know why?"

"No. Why?"

Russell leaned into me so he could whisper. We halted before a display where two people wearing what looked like black wetsuits gave some kind of demonstration. He stroked my right arm with one finger, which made me a bit uncomfortable. Goosebumps rose on my flesh, and he said, "Skin comes from the same embryological ectoderm as the eyes, so it's all a matter of bringing out a latent sensitivity that's already there. It's like meditation. Some people have the mind for it, and some don't."

"You use your mind to relay info from your skin to your optical nerves?"

He shot me a pointer finger. "You learn fast." He stood aside and looked to the two people in wetsuits who still had their backs to one another. They touched themselves in pattering little motions. Their touch wasn't sexual, but was more percussive like Morse code. "It's crawl, walk, run. I'm running. They're crawling."

One of them heard him, and took the opportunity to stop tapping his chest and flick Russell the bird. My friend didn't take offense. "I love you, too, Michael." His wide stoner smile remained plastered on his face, and he spoke to me from the crooked corner of his mouth. "The skin can identify pressure at intervals of about one ten-thousandth of a second."

"What's the rate for eyes?"

He seemed pleased to see that I was still thinking in terms of eye-skin analogies. The music segued to a mixture of war's blitzkrieg sounds and the squeal a pig might make if it was still alive when a saw was taken to its form in an abattoir. "The eye can discriminate at about thirty-five thousandths of a second, in the cases of the most perceptive."

"Like you?" I asked.

He blushed from the compliment, but didn't argue. "What they're really doing is practicing, trying to see if they can get the skin to reach sensory parity with the eye." He looked away from me, and back to the exhibitors in wetsuits. I looked closer and saw the one on the right was female, with pert breasts jutting from her form-fitting wetsuit. "Good luck," Russell said, and motioned for me to follow him farther into his domain.

"Enough cutaneous communication," he said. "Let's get a bit more esoteric."

We came to a corner of the hangar where a man with a broadly muscled back was tethered to metal grillwork. Two women stood on either side of their prisoner, both wearing black brocade corsets and nun habits. One woman applied a cat-o-nine tails to the man's spine, creating whip marks that reddened the flesh.

Russell could tell I was underwhelmed, and he said, "Just wait." His eyes were shining. The woman on the right stopped whipping, and the one on the left extended the blade on a Stanley knife and made a crosshatching network of cuts up and down the man's back. His muscles tensed, twitched imperceptibly as they bled a bit.

The woman on the left retracted the Exact-o blade and waited with her sister. The man's bald head shined like shellac in the strobe light. He now began to strain. I thought he might be reacting in pain to what had been done to his back, or that perhaps he was trying to break free from his bondage. I learned otherwise as I saw that his straining was causing the cuts to raise wheals on his back. What looked like slices in the flesh a moment ago now took on the look of three-dimensional mountain ranges on a map.

"It's self-induced vagotonia," Russell said to me. The moment the cuts became fully-formed welts, the two women leaned in close and touched the former knife and whip-marks. They scrutinized the wounds like tarot cards that would tell them the date of their death. "The whip and the razor provide the initial stimulation," Russell said.

He walked forward, and the two women who'd been crowding the man like suckling vampires now moved back to let the ringmaster get a look. "The rest is done by Marcus." Russell patted the tied man on his bald head. He spoke to the man. "Tell him how you do it, Marcus."

"Yes, sir, Mr. Nadler." I suspected Russell Nadler wasn't a stickler for such honorifics. I also thought Marcus got off on his submissiveness whether what was being done to him also served a secondary, augury function. Marcus strained his neck and his trap muscles flared like he was pumping iron. He spoke to me while holding that uncomfortable pose. "I didn't know I had the gift until Mr. Nadler sent me to the chop shop. They did some acupuncture on me and found out I had a hyper-reactive vagus nerve. Wasn't none of my doing, just genetics." He paused and shivered from pain, ecstasy, or both. "I found out when I got a hard-on from pain that I could make the fluid move from the capillaries into my skin, and that people who were smart enough could see things in the skin."

One of the women spoke to me, wiping a smudged bit of black lipstick from her face. "It's basically dermographic tea leaf readings."

"Or I-Ching yarrow stalks written on his back," her sister said.

Marcus faced forward where he was tied, although he spoke to me while staring through the dark grates of the dungeon grating. "My skin's right about two-thirds of the time. I could work for bookies or something, but I'd rather be here with Mr. Nadler."

"And we appreciate you," Russell said. He nodded to the two gothic women once, and then bade me to follow him. I was getting antsy, and I think he sensed it. We walked until we stood before a cast iron chamber. It looked like a modded single-occupancy sleeper coffin, although it was ribbed and shaped more like a lone hexagonal cell from a honeycomb.

"That a sensory dep chamber?"

That made him laugh and flash his goofy discolored choppers again. "Quite the opposite, actually."

I knew I was out of my element and decided not to venture any more guesses, although all of this was not totally alien to me. We had employed a psychic back when I was at SPD years ago, especially on missing person cases. That was usually a desperation move, not something I was eager to make into a cult.

A volute of what looked like dry ice billowed from beneath the machine and cast those hovering around it into greenish shadows. The fog drifted over us, and I coughed as Rus explained. "It's a synesthesia chamber. Are you acquainted with it?"

I stopped coughing like someone who'd taken their first shisha hit and said, "Synesthesia, yes. The chamber, no."

"It converts one sense to another, although one can never predict which sense the chamber will play with."

"It's heuristic?" I asked.

"It searches for fears, weaknesses, and then reflects those back to you. Whichever sense you're least acquainted with or comfortable with experiencing in an expanded manner is the one it hones in on and magnifies."

So it was heuristic and sadistic. "Why does it do that?"

"To teach you about yourself. It's cross-modal transfer, flooding in cognitive-behavioral terms. I've heard it's quite the trip."

"You haven't done it yourself?"

He folded his arms over his chest. "You have to train for a year or so and become good at transcendental meditation before you can even think of testing yourself in there."

The door on the front of the machine opened, emitting a pressurized hiss and lowering by means of hydraulics. "What happens if you fail the test?" I didn't think I was ready to hear color or taste sound.

"You lose your mind." Russell uncrossed his arms. A darkened form rushed out of the chamber into the understanding arms of attendants, who wrapped her in a terrycloth towel. She wept and wailed.

"Did she fail?" I asked.

"No," Russell said, and walked forward. I walked with him. "If she had, she'd be catatonic now. If they're not in the fetal position after the hatch opens, they've had a good session."

I looked at the form being wiped down with the towel. She was slicked in some sort of plasmatic afterbirth, but despite her distress I could see it was Viva Jasmine. Her hair was the same royal purple as it was in her mugshot, although it was styled different. It was plastered in icicle shapes rather than in severe, asymmetrical bangs. It made me think she had root mods rather than a dye job, since those fickle enough to dye usually changed their hair color often.

She looked up at me with warm doe eyes, moon-shaped like those of a living anime character. The angles of her face were soft and round. "Oh God," she said, and shivered. The voice didn't match the face, which appeared as young as or maybe younger than the one in the mugshot. She sounded like a torch singer whose voice was raspy with whiskey, cigarettes, and heartbreak. Yet she looked like a teenager, aside from the feature of her teardrop breasts that were as heavy with milk as those of Ms. Boxer.

"Ms. Jasmine?" I asked.

"She can't hear you," one of her friends drying her with the towel said.

I looked over at Russell. "What-"

"It was a hormonal inhibitor," he said. "She was modded to stay in early pubescence. A lot of her clientele were hebephiliacs but they didn't want to do time in the Stone Schengen just because they like adolescent girls."

"Should be castrated," one of her female friends said, rubbing her shoulders. Viva cried and a snot bubble popped from her nose. I looked back to Russell. "How often can someone do this?"

"It's not recommended to go to the well more than once a year."

"She does it once a month or so," her friend said, caressing Viva's trembling shoulder. "She's a trooper."

"Jesus," I said.

Russell leaned into me and whispered, "She's no good to you in this state. When she recovers, I'll give her whatever you want to subvoc to me now and relay it to her."

"Do you have a piece of paper?" A couple of those guiding Viva through her comedown laughed at my Luddite ways.

Russell was a bit cleverer, and winked with one of his three eyes. "Trying to practice our cursive, are we?"

CHAPTER NINE

VICE SQUAD MEMORIES

Gyrocopters were forbidden in Green Node fly space, and I couldn't see what the hell the gunmetal craft was doing floating through an area with no helipad. My confusion came to an end a moment later, as the strength of the rotors grew and partiers and late night strollers ran in every direction away from the copter trying to land. I hid behind a shade tree illumined by the moon.

I didn't know what the hell was up, but I didn't have my piece on my person to defend myself. I'd given Russell Nadler a letter to give to Viva Jasmine whenever she awakened from her stupor, and I was planning on going home to shower and shoot the breeze with Denholm before this whirlybird came from nowhere.

A unicyclist appeared on the sidewalk. I'd seen him earlier sipping a latte with heavy foam in front of the café. He dismounted his wheel and walked up a man in a navy trench coat that barely concealed his no-go zone patrol armor. I recognized the undergarment's bulk from my time wearing the light mesh myself while on meat beat a long time ago.

"You're not allowed to be here in that thing!" The cyclist pointed at the gyrocopter.

I placed the thug quickly as one of Vasily Timofev's foot soldiers. He flashed a right handing glinting with a duster implant and swung a wide looping hook that shattered the unicyclist's helmet as if it was made of asbestos. A short yelp left the biker's mouth and he lay curled in a concussed pile on the concrete. Anyone else who had thoughts of criticizing the new arrivals scattered to the tree line.

Unfortunately the chrome-fisted thug spotted me hiding behind the oak. "You, get your ass in the copter. Now."

"Moving." I let loose the trunk of the oak and stepped over the conked cyclist.

"Aren't you worried about being followed?" I asked. It was as much protest as I had the balls to offer.

The flunky tapped a metal tube extending from the side of the hawk's carriage, and because his hand was partially metal there was a hollow *thunk*. "We've got vector thrust capabilities once we're airborne."

"Impressive."

The gear talk seemed to make him less hostile, and he grunted before elaborating. "Yeah, push comes to shove and SPD climbs up our asses, the rotors can fold and we can go fixed wing."

I stepped aboard and seated myself in a contoured leather seat that was heated. The crime boss Vasily Timofev sat next to me, and stared out the window at the expanse of park and greenspace extending into the distance. He didn't seem much interested in me, despite the pains he'd taken to locate me and scoop me up. I wondered what he wanted, but I knew better than to press him.

He motioned with his finger toward the pilot ahead of us, and we lifted off. He spoke now, perhaps as much to his thug as to me. "I don't like the Green Node very much, I must confess."

His accent was as strong as it had been when I'd picked him up as a minor enforcer in Maskaev's crew. I gathered from the size of the bird that his days of splitting skulls for others were in the rearview.

"It's not bad," I said, bracing as we took off. The engine was whisper-quiet, and we lifted into the night sky. "I got a pretty good espresso earlier."

"Yes, but the trees don't glow."

"They don't like bioluminescents," I said. "They think they look pretty, but they don't like it when the glow buds get picked up by the wind and end up in their food."

"Can't blame them," the big guy to my left said. "Nobody wants their shit to glow in the dark." I still couldn't put a name to the face. He patted me on the fleshy joint of my left shoulder that linked to my cybered arm. "I'm glad you came along willingly."

We flew between two skyscrapers and headed toward a red-blinking radio tower in the distance. It looked like we were going to fly above the zoned area and into the Edge. I didn't want to show my fear, so I tried idle chitchat with the muscle. "And what would you have done if I didn't come along?"

He pulled out an Uzi mini-auto with a rotary trigger mechanism. He stroked its compound plastic and said, "I would have aired you out."

I thought that being clipped might be better than getting socked like that unicyclist. If the guy was lucky, he'd wake six hours later in Schengen Med with a needle draining his subdural hematoma.

"Put the gun away," Vasily said. He pulled a golden medallion from inside of his velour tracksuit. The outfit was orange except for some white piping. The color reminded me of the carpet on the casino floor at the Zhakpot when an obstinate vomit stain refused to come out and faded instead.

Vasily stroked the crown of thorns on his Jesus piece necklace. "I suppose I love the lights of the city because I grew up in a small village in Kazakhstan with no electricity." He looked at me. "When you want for something when you are young, you can never get enough of it when you're older."

"I imagine you've got the credits," I said.

We banked over the campus of Schengen Tech. A shuttle shaped like a giant white pill floated through the night, taking students to their midnight classes. Vasily winked at me. "You jealous?"

"Not really. I can sleep well at night. Clear conscience and all that."

He waved off my moralizing. "Stop talking like a cop. You're a house dick now, yes?"

"Yes."

"But you're on another case?"

I shrugged. "It fell into my lap."

We crossed the border into the Edge. It was my first time there in years, only now I wasn't in a flying "V" formation with a tactical extraction squad. I felt naked, despite the state-of-the-art bird I was flying in and even though I was in the company of killers. Vasily Timofev was a shrewd gangster who'd managed to navigate his way through the underworld with the viciousness of a bareknuckle brawler and the intellect of a chess master. No one was hard enough to control what went on out in the Edge, though.

He sensed my fear and his cold eyes glowed like a blade catching the light just right. "Relax." He leaned forward and tapped the pilot. "My friend is modded six ways to Sunday and his reflexes got him Olympic gold before I had him tailored."

I decided not to look down anyway, although the glow from flaming oil drums and burning buildings was strong enough to cast all four of our faces in reddish tint even this high in the sky. He played some more with his Jesus piece, and caught me eyeing it. "You like?"

"I couldn't get away with wearing it, but it works for you."

He didn't do irony, but he didn't have to. Vasily stuffed the gold amulet back into the ample chest hairs jutting above the half-zipped velour jacket. "I am going to talk to you for a moment, and I want you to listen. When I ask you a question, you may speak. Do you understand?"

"Yes," I said.

"If you attempt to record or subvoc while I speak and Ruslan catches you, he will beat you senseless, break your nose, and throw you out of our helicopter. Do you understand?"

"I won't use my mods or ER."

"Do you understand?" He repeated.

"Yes."

"Good." He played with the gold chain of his piece, which was as thick as that used to tether a fighting bulldog. He glanced out of the window. The copter lurched. I stared down with him, toward the tops of tenements. I looked at the burnt shells of buildings where a lone mad soul was playing parkour in a condemned co-op, hopping from fire escape to chimney to windowsill.

"I read a lot while I was in prison," Vasily said. "I never touched dope, except to sell it." He stroked his chin. He was deep in contemplation, in another place while still here with me. "I was never curious about it you know, until I read *The Odyssey*. Do you know it?"

I stowed the urge to check the tens of thousands of books I had indexed in my head. I didn't want to go back on my word by using my mods now, and get thrown from a helicopter for trying to win a trivia game with a Kazak drug lord. Nevertheless, he'd asked a question and I didn't want to piss him off. "I think I've read it," I finally said.

"'Whoever drinks a drop thereof, on that day no tear would fall down his cheeks, not even if his mother and father died, not even if men slew his brother or dear son with the sword, before his own eyes.'" He looked over at me now. His cold eyes were welling with tears. That didn't make them any less cold.

"My brother was killed, head chopped off by rebels in Chechnya."

I stowed the urge to offer my condolences. He would see through them.

He had to know that I knew the kinds of things he was involved in, and that I didn't care about him or his family. "I used…" He held up a single finger on his left hand. "One time. Just once, after my brother's death." His voice was now a whisper. "And the pain was gone." He made a gesture with his right hand, an indeterminate grasp for fading ether. "But the pain came back an hour later. Then I knew the drug was a lie, and that people who used it were both weak and stupid." His momentary vulnerability was gone. "Coleridge was wrong. There is no milk of paradise." He pointed toward the scorched ghetto beneath us. "Not at least on this side of the grave. Perhaps my brother has found something like peace now that he is dead, though."

He stared toward the purple clouds above us for a moment and said, "My Tasmanian contacts had been producing a motherlode of altered poppies, and they found a way to double the strength of the opium by manufacturing poppy straw concentrate. It was much stronger than the other stuff and much more compact. Thus it was easier to smuggle. Do you understand?"

"Yes," I said.

The chopper did a one-eighty. "My sources have dried up due to a host of issues, some relating to eradication efforts, the changing of political winds, and for other reasons that are none of your concern."

I didn't blame him for not elaborating. I didn't know how long his goons had been shadowing me, but they may have seen me talking to some of my old buddies on the force like Lieutenant Dear. An ex-cop wasn't ever totally ex.

"It has come to our attention that you are pursuing someone with *extremely* advanced pharmacological abilities. This is the kind of person who could not only help me reclaim one of my most lucrative streams of revenue, but could perhaps increase my power in Schengen City." His cold eyes grew harder. I doubted he had any mods. He didn't need them. "If I don't get my hands on this exceptional individual and one of my rivals does, it could seriously weaken my position. My place in the order is already tenuous."

I nodded. I wondered where or how he had found out about the sample currently marinating in Lazlo's petri dish. Maybe he had a remote relay stored in a little wooden nutcracker curio in the Wonder Chamber in Chinatown. For all I knew, he could have been running a tap through Ducky's rubberized bowels.

Vasily sensed the gears working in my mind, and waved his hand as if the gesture could unclutter the thoughts from my head and bring me back to focus on his particular piece of the puzzle. "Just as you needn't know every aspect of my trade, I needn't know every aspect of your affairs. I will not pry." I believed him. I knew him to be obsessed with honor, impervious to interrogation; he'd remained stoic after everything from good cop/bad cop to torture had been tried on him when we pressed him for details about Maskaev's operations. That he'd possibly had a hand in his boss's murder didn't mean that he would be willing to rat him out to us.

The glow of my own Node Sweet Node reflected across the bubble windshield of the gyrocopter. We glided over the Sphinx and edged perilously close to the Eifel Tower. Vasily's mood brightened now that we were back among the neon and bioluminescence, a colorful mixture of tropical fish tank glow and perennial New Year's Eve glitter. "I love lights," he said, and smiled.

His super-stud pilot glided toward the Zhakpot's helipad. Vasily squared himself to me. "Solve your case. Find your cheating husband or your missing daughter or whatever pot of gold you're chasing." He pulled his golden Christ back from underneath his tracksuit jacket and stroked it like a Baoding ball. "But whenever you turn up the identity of whoever made that beautiful drug, you give that name to me and only me. Otherwise I'll have Ruslan strip you naked, hang you upside down, and cut you in half with a saw. We'll start at your balls and keep cutting until we go through the top of your head. It will be done slow."

The gyro finally touched down. Kryptonite green kliegs shot toward the sky like searchlights, reminding gamblers of the allure of greed that had existed since paper money times.

"Have a good night, Detective Moglich." Vasily Timofev had exhausted his audience with me. He stared out the window, toward a hot-air balloon lumbering through the sky. Its glowing panels spelled out a message in rose red gilded in track lighting. It said, "Jennifer and Jonathan are getting married."

"It is quite romantic," he observed.

"Okay," Ruslan said. "Out."

He opened the door, and I took my cue. Vasily's voice came to me over the whap of the rotors slicing through the muggy night air. "Good luck."

I didn't have the strength left for words, and my rubbery legs barely carried me toward the rooftop entrance of the hotel. I walked toward the door. The bird took off behind me, kicking up dust that soaked into my clothes and would give fits to the in-house dry cleaner's.

Being threatened with torture was never fun, but at least the Kazak kingpin hadn't given me an ultimatum of the find-this-guy-or-you're-dead variety. I was also thankful for the small mercy that he didn't want to pry into the other elements of the ongoing investigation. But it was nice to know I was of some use to someone who had a streak for killing people when he felt they outlived their usefulness.

Things were quite complicated already, but they could have been much worse. It went without saying that I would need something stronger than Kahlua for my nightcap. Denholm would have to tranquilize me with more than whale songs and cresting foam tide tonight. He would also be doing triple duty as shrink, confidant, and bartender. I pitied the poor machine, waved my fingerprints over the rooftop door, and waited for the red LED to flash green.

CHAPTER TEN

LIGHT LUNCH IN BOMBAYBERG

A message came in the night, informing me that Kyra Boxer was still alive. She was still asleep at the Ming, but she was also for all intents and purposes dead to the world and deep in a coma. Another more promising message came from Viva Jasmine early the next morning as the sun was rising. She wanted to meet me for lunch in Bombayberg.

I packed my Federated Arms peashooter "bitch gun," as Lieutenant Dear would have called it if he caught me wearing it. I wasn't even sure what I was trying to prove by packing her. If Vasily came for my head, I was dead. If the mastermind behind Blankstone's murder wanted me out of the picture, I would be erased in short order. Maybe the piece was just a security blanket, my own worrying stone to ease me through troubling times.

I caught the first maglev running. Once I hit Bombay Main, I hired out an automated rickshaw. I found myself carried past salmon-colored buildings painted soft honey by the sunlight filtering through the sun-splashed palm trees. The rickshaw halted in front of the takeout eatery where Viva Jasmine had told me to meet her. I swiped my sticker over the rickshaw's sensor and got out.

She was waiting for me below the great folly of a building. It was a sixteen-story glazed brick pagoda topped by a multi-armed blue Kali with her tongue sticking out and a severed head in each one of her hands. The gore was too pretty for me to be disturbed by it, rich and garish in blues and reds.

Viva Jasmine wore a tasteful dolphin-blue bell skirt cinched by a belt as wide as a schoolmarm's paddle and the same rich brown. She squinted through the sunlight, and used her right hand as a visor to get a better look at me. "Are you the one who wrote me the note?"

"Yes, ma'am, I am." I walked toward her.

"Cute," she said, and extended her hand. The first letter in the tattoo grafted above her left breast segued from "V" to "D."

She noticed my scrutiny and covered the tat. "Don't judge me. I was high."

"I've seen much worse," I said.

"Yeah but if you're going to do anything shady, it's best not to have any 'identifying marks.'" She made air quotes by forming pincers with her pointer and middle fingers. Then she turned from me, back to the window of the pagoda before I could say anything else. She took her food and waved her sticker over the turbaned man's pay station, and then she clicked a full credit into the tip cup.

"Generous," I said.

"Karma."

She walked under the shade of the palms and I walked alongside her. I looked at what she was eating, some sort of white broth with thick strands of coconut flesh swimming in a bowl fashioned from a banana leaf. It smelled of chutney and mango.

"You want some?" She blew on the steaming broth, and took a tentative sip. The point of her tongue was scalded for her efforts.

I shook my head. She stared at the shadows our forms made as we walked, and then spoke, "Not too many people I know can write cursive anymore."

"It's a lost art," I allowed.

"I've heard some people can do math in their heads. That shit is crazy."

"Takes all kinds."

She held out her bowl toward all of Bombayberg. "I love this Node."

"Do you like the Green Node?"

She shrugged, and I noticed she had a light smattering of freckles on the exposed flesh of her neck and shoulders. "I go there for Russell's events."

"How often does he have them?"

"Nightly, almost every night of the week I mean." She coughed, tried her soup again, and found it to her liking. "You just came on a really weird night."

"You've got balls to step into that machine. I wouldn't do it."

She smiled at that. "Well, *this* is unfair. You saw me at my most vulnerable, and I don't have any dirt on you."

"I'm too boring to have any dirt. I'm a house dick at the Zhakpot."

She laughed so hard that she snorted a bit of coconut milk and then covered her mouth. "The Eurotrash resort?"

"Don't knock it," I said. "We've got our own volcano."

"Shitcano." She continued giggling.

"Don't tell the tourists."

We turned a corner. She spotted a bench, exhaling mightily as she went to sit on it. "I'm sorry," she said. "I'm a lazy heifer."

"No problem."

I sat next to her on the bench. She stared in the direction of a pond where ducks swam and people threw breadcrumbs. "On the subject of dirt then, I'm guessing you saw my file?"

"Nothing to be ashamed of." I shook my head.

"The record says 'opiate' but that makes it seem like heroin or something."

I leaned forward. "It wasn't?" She shook her head. "What was it, then?"

"Opium," she said, "Literally, it wasn't a derivative."

I thought about something. "So when you're in that synesthesia chamber, do you ever get flashbacks?"

She had finished her soup, and searched around for a trashcan. Not finding one, she threw the banana leaf down and crushed it under the heel of her leather sandal. "It's biodegradable."

"What isn't, these days?"

She stifled a belch, and I was slightly aroused. It had been years since I'd dated, but I'd always been attracted to women with healthy appetites. "What do you mean by flashbacks?" she asked.

"Opium gives you crazy dreams, doesn't it? I would think that with your history, that going into that chamber thing you might be susceptible to-"

She shook her head and her purple bangs remained still, stiff with product. "Opium dreams aren't really like that. They're pretty things you kind of see out of the corner of your eye. But if you look carefully or try to touch them, they go away."

Her voice trailed off, as if just thinking about falling off the tail of the dragon made her want to chase it one last time. "I never saw myself when I was stoned, but I'm pretty sure you don't even go into REM sleep on opium. The dreams aren't even dreams."

Nothing in my GenMed mod was confirming or denying what she said. She sensed me staring into the implant in my brain. "Stop that," she said, chastising me slightly.

"Sorry," I said. "Force of habit."

"Opium's a minor addiction compared to some mods."

"I won't argue with you there."

She tucked a strand of her glowing purple hair behind her ear. I looked down at her tat again. "Stop that," she said.

"Sorry." I looked upward, toward a bird chirping in its nest on the branch of the tree directly above us.

"You don't have to look up at the sky." She giggled again, a titter as light and frail as the song of the bird. "You can look me in the eye. Just don't look at my tat, or my tits."

She adjusted something beneath her sky-blue top, and there was a slick suctioning sound. I looked away, over her shoulder. "Excuse me," she said. "I'm leaking and I don't want to ruin another dress, especially not this one. I just got it from Bayside Imports."

"It's pretty," I said, and since she had mentioned the dress again I had a pretext to sneak glances at her.

Her fingers played in the dark space of her cleavage. She removed something from the nipple of her left breast, its flesh tone so seamlessly matching her own skin that I didn't realize she was peeling something away until it was completely free. She held the milk-saturated breast pad up to me, suction-side first. I could feel its warmth as she held it in front of my eyes.

"It's medical grade silicon," she said, and then replaced it on the breast. "I've got silicon *in* my tits and on them."

"Kyra used seashells."

She looked at me like I was a boyfriend who'd made a hideous faux pas during the first meal with her parents. "What?"

I remained silent, not sure of how or where I screwed up but nevertheless certain that I had erred somewhere. The bird in the tree above us stopped chirping.

"How do you know Kyra?"

I shifted on the bench. "Her friend hired me to find out who hurt her."

"Hurt!" She was shouting. "Punched, sexually assaulted, raped? Can we do specifics here?"

I stood, grabbed her by the arm, and led her along the sunbaked gravel pathway. "Keep your voice down," I whispered. "There are some heavy hitters involved here, and too much scrutiny means I lose my ass and maybe you lose yours too."

She looked around the park, as if she suspected now that we were being followed. It wouldn't have surprised me, although both our biter and the Kazak had enough money to do their spying through remote toys rather than through a man.

I released her arm. "I'm sorry," I said. She remained silent and hugged her arms over her leaking breasts. "Your friend Kyra Boxer was attacked by someone. She's alive and seemingly stable, but she's unconscious."

"Where?"

I shook my head. "I can't reveal details about a client. Suffice it to say that your friend is safe." I glanced around us, at the alternating patches of sun and shade in the park. "She's probably safer than us." I stopped walking. "I would like to find out who hurt her, and I would like you to help me."

"Okay."

"I need you to answer some questions."

She laughed. "So you won't answer my questions, and you want me to answer yours?"

"Yes," I said, and I felt my blood pressure rising. "That's how investigations work."

"I feel like I'm back in the SPD interrogation room." She held out her upturned arms. "You want to check for track marks, officer?"

I wasn't interested in her theatrics. "Tell me why you and your friend are lactating. I know you're not pregnant, so why are you modded and who did the modding?" I paused to catch my breath and suppress my rising bile. I thought that losing my temper might have lost her to the investigation, but my distress seemed to prove to her that I was at least human.

"I can answer your first question. I don't know the answer to your second one."

"You don't know who modded you?" I found that hard to believe. Most modifications took three to six hours. The rapport between modder and moddee was similar to that between a tattoo artist working his Needlegun and a client. One tended to talk to the person making permanent changes to their bodies. Questions about aftercare and safety were pretty much par for the course.

"I was blindfolded," Viva said.

"When you were modded?"

She nodded. I asked, "How about Kyra? Was she blindfolded?"

80

"No." We started walking again, and Viva whispered, "Stand in front of me for a moment."

I did as I was told, and she adjusted the latex cups over breasts. "My boobies are on fire."

I laughed, somehow thrown off-guard by the childish and yet sexually arousing word she used. She smiled at me, a look of maternal pity on her strangely young face. I remembered Russ Nadler explaining to me that due to her mod she would have that strangely teenaged look for the remainder of her life. I tried not to think about how the mod would wear as she aged, how a woman in her sixties designed to look sixteen forever might hold up.

I felt bad enough for her to cry, but I had an investigation to run, a genius psycho to catch, and a drug dealer to mollify. "So Kyra never told you who did the mod?"

"That's right," Viva said. "She never told any of us."

She'd finished adjusting her breast cups, and I stopped setting the pick for her. We started walking again, slowly. "Us?"

"I didn't know the identities of the other girls involved in this. She kept us in the dark about each other, and about him."

"Him, who?"

We stopped walking again.

She threw her hands up, huffing in exasperation. "I just told you I didn't know his fucking name. I couldn't even peek at his face while he modded us."

"Okay," I lowered my voice, and tried to talk her down like a potential suicide on a penthouse balcony. "What was the mod?"

She lowered her own voice to match mine now. "I think it might be too kinky and weird for you."

I waved off her concern. "I worked sex crimes. If children or animals weren't involved, I really don't give a shit."

"Well," she debated how to phrase it. "The men wanted to be children. ABDL."

I was like everyone else in our society in that I had twenty-four hour, permanent access to pornography in my head. I was familiar with the fetish. "Adult baby, diaper lovers." I spoke low. If we'd been at the party with the leather-clad Goth girls in corsets I might have spoken louder, but we were in the middle of Bombayberg. "What's the big deal?"

There was something I wasn't getting, and her lips were curled in frustration. "It was ABDL with a twist." I waited for her to tell me what the twist was. Instead, she asked me a question. "You have mods, right?"

"Yeah, I'm at about twenty percent."

"I'm only fifteen," she said, a trace of moral superiority in her voice. Some people thought they were better because they had more mods. Others thought they were better because they had less. Pretty much everyone thought they were better for one reason or another. I waited. She said, "You know you have to get tested before you get mods, to check your aptitude, make sure it will take, and that you're not allergic?"

"Yes," I said.

"Well, before Uncle Creepy modded us he had Kyra run some tests."

"Uncle Creepy?"

"That's what I call him."

"I can't say I blame you."

An Indian family out for a Sunday stroll walked past us, and we held our tongues until they walked by. "Anyway," Viva said, "I let Kyra do a blood draw on me. She said that if the results came back positive, I could make good money playing mommy for rich men who would pay well to get treated like babies." She burped again from the coconut soup and resumed. "I would get a breast implant to carry milk, let them nurse, and then get paid. It sounded easy enough."

"Was it?"

She smirked. "I don't want to get into the particulars of my profession, and what's more I don't want to judge anyone."

"I'm not here to judge anyone, either. I'm here to find some things out."

"No," she said, "To answer your question, it was not easy. It was gross. I had to change diapers full of grown man shit. My sister has a nephew and baby shit doesn't smell anywhere near as bad as man shit."

I felt bad for her, and for any other woman in her line of work. Taking money was supposed to somehow absolve one from the perversions of the paying customer, but it always eventually ended up implicating the women and making them more like the men. It made them in essence one with the men, and mocking or judging their clients didn't change anything. They had traded something substantial for money, another kind of virginity.

"There were perks," she said, brightening. "There still are."

"Like?"

"Remember I said we got a blood test?"

"Yes."

She walked closer to me, so that I could smell the aloe gel on the pads wicking to her sore breasts. "Maybe it was the opium I'd done that left its residue in my system, but I was cleared by the blood test. I turned out to have the right kind of metabolism for the mod."

"What kind is that?"

"The kind that can rapidly transform codeine to morphine." She gripped her ample breasts, massaging them proudly notwithstanding that we were in public. I looked around, seeing if anyone from a prude to a pervert would notice. Most people were engaged in their own lazy Sunday idylls. I thought maybe she was crazy. "The men aren't just getting milk from the mod. They're getting a drug. A drug no one else is getting."

"It's a new cultivar," I said, thinking of Lazlo in his toyshop.

"But it's not just the men who get the effects of the drug." She let go of her breasts, and they bounced heavily before growing still. I was grateful that she was no longer fondling herself in public. A sleepy smile drifted across her face, an opiated cloud that seemed to carry her away and that troubled me as much as it pleased her. "I get high every time baby sucks mommy's titty. Some opium for baby, some opium for mommy."

My skin crawled. I experienced a wash of emotions, ranging from some infantile core hidden in man that she exposed with her practiced baby talk to embarrassment that she had forgotten she was in public. I was now implicated in her antics. I grabbed her arm again and steered her around the circular path, whispering to her like a cuckolded husband embarrassed by her open flirtation with other men.

"Bernard Blankstone," I said, and my words brought her back to the present like cold water or a slap to the face.

"What do you know about him?"

Time to take a stab in the dark. "He was one of Kyra's clients."

Viva bit her lower lip, as if that could help her remain silent. She released the lip from her teeth and said, "We're not allowed to reveal the names of clients."

"There's no use protecting the identity of a dead man."

"No, but it's important to protect his name and his reputation. It's important to protect his memory."

"Why should he have been ashamed? Everyone doesn't go to the civic center on vanilla night."

"Cute," she said, and stroked my ear with her left hand. I batted the hand away. "You don't understand," she said.

"I agree with you."

"Rich and powerful men have so much stress, so much responsibility. To give up control and be a baby for only an hour a week, it gives them so much relief and pleasure."

"So what's the problem?"

She reached over to me and patted my gun tucked under my clamshell. "You were a cop, right?"

"Good guess."

We had done a full circuit, and were now back to the pagoda that smelled of tandoori and was topped by the blue goddess. "If a cop sees a shrink even if the department says it's okay, it still makes him look bad. It makes him look weak, right?"

I wondered if she had any cops among her clients. She obviously catered more to the well-to-do, but I was curious about the price of her services or at least how much the opiated milk cost. "You're right," I conceded. "You look weak if you see a shrink, like you can't handle the pressure."

"Same thing with the big timers like Blankstone. If you're the kind of guy who is responsible for billions in dark coin transactions and you're also the most famous starchitect in the Nodes, people want to know they can trust you. If you're a whale of that size and you wake up with the flu one morning, it affects markets in Reykjavik. What happens when it gets out that you're sucking an untested, unpatented drug synthesized in a breast mod made in a back-alley butcher shop?"

I wondered how much she knew about financial markets, instruments, derivatives, and the like just based on what men let slip from their lips before or after her milk was drying on their mouths. She closed her eyes, stumbled once. I wondered if maybe she had a leak, if she wasn't in fact somehow high on herself.

She stopped before the curb and held out her hand to flag down an auto-rickshaw. I caught up to her and asked, "Where are you going?"

"Home," she said. "To express milk." She stood in place and hotfooted as if she had to pee badly. "My titties hurt when they get too engorged." She looked at me. "Do you want to come?"

"What?"

She smiled coyly. "Nightcap. The milk has to come out one way or the other." She flicked her wrist at me dismissively. "I know you're all man, that the diaper game isn't your thing. Still, you can get high off the milk."

A rickshaw pulled to the curb. She pulled her sticker out, waving for the fare and giving a second wand wave for the tip. It was good karma, as she said. She opened the door and turned back to me one last time. "Businessmen billionaires aren't the only ones dealing with stress. I imagine you could use a breather."

"That's okay," I said. I didn't have the heart to tell her that in addition to carrying the opium and the milk in her mammary glands, she might also be carrying some sort of gorgon-headed parasite in her bosom. And there was little that could be done to bring attention to the problem. If I went into SPD headquarters with this story and started spilling my guts, Vasily Timofev would have me offed from the inside via a Cyrillic kite telling his brothers to shank me. Even if I did manage to tell the cops the story, I knew I stood a good chance of being considered nuts and ending up in a straightjacket. Then all my mods would be deactivated and I would be cut off from the outside world.

"You go ahead," I said. "I don't want to hold you up and I definitely don't want you to ruin that dress." She smiled at me, and I had to avert my eyes from her strangely childlike face mounted on that buxom frame.

"Stay in touch," she said, getting into the rickshaw's wicker-laced backseat. "When you find something out, let me know."

"I will," I promised. I hoped to solve this thing soon, to capture the "Uncle Creepy" behind it all. I would press him for the recipe for the drug, and press him for some sort of antidote for the parasite. Then I would turn him over to SPD, or maybe he would have an "accident" and plummet from the roof of the Zhakpot while we were struggling for possession of my peashooter.

I would have to catch him first, though. I waited for Viva/Diva Jasmine's rickshaw to pull out, and then stuck out my arm to hail my own ride.

CHAPTER ELEVEN

NO PEACE IN THE NIGHT

The Goldmine was a Texas saloon-themed restaurant on the ground plaza of the Zhakpot. It had good synth sirloin. Its batwing doors let in ambient sounds from the casino floor, but the steakhouse was at least a good quarter-mile away from the slot machines.

The kitchen was down to a skeleton crew after midnight. Everyone knew me as the house dick though, so they agreed to seat me in a corner booth and grille me a sirloin in blackened onions. I sipped an Irish coffee and listened to the player pianoforte hammer away standards on itself.

I took another drink, and thought some about the case. It seemed possible to me that either Kyra Boxer or someone spying on her decided to make the most of the knowledge of Blankstone's fetish. The details were sketchy, but blackmail was probably involved. The billionaire had called their bluff, and lost his head literally because of his stubbornness. Why Kyra had been attacked and how Viva Jasmine fit into this were still details that had to be worked out, and I wasn't sure how much time I had left.

A server burst through the kitchen doors and walked to my table with a steak on a plate. "Howdy, partner!" He wore chaps and a shirt with a cactus patterned on it.

"Thank you," I said, and dug in. He turned and headed back toward the kitchen, his spurs rattling as he went.

"You think that thing's real?"

I looked up. Lieutenant Dear was standing there. He couldn't even wait for me to cut into the marbled meat. "Ten percent at most," I said. "I eat a real Kobe steak about once a year."

"I know the steak ain't one-hundred percent real meat." He shifted into the booth next to me, and looked above the player piano. "I meant those."

86

He pointed toward some tchotchkes nailed to the wall on a rawhide tarp. There was a cow skull and a branding iron.

"I could get one of those antiquarian mods installed and then have a look see."

"'Have a look see.' You even talk like a cowpoke when you're in here."

The piano segued to *Home on the Range*, and a couple of drunks joined in. I rolled my eyes.

"How's the Zhakpot treating you?"

I ignored his words, tore into the steak, and chewed. I spoke around a mouthwatering bit of the faux steak. "I found a maid stealing complimentary mints last week. She had a whole black market going."

"Can't trust those Edgers."

Denholm's Queen's English reached my ear, and my brain had to do double duty listening to him and Dear. "Sir, self-cleaning of black tie, grey striped trousers, and morning coat currently underway. I will be unavailable for the next thirty minutes."

"Thank you, Denholm."

"It's rude to subvoc at the table."

I winked at Dear. "Sorry, mother."

He didn't smile, which made me think we were dispensed with the preliminaries and he was about to drop a bomb. "Homicide caught a body last night."

I cut another slice from my steak. "And?" I didn't want to sound callous, but someone or other got murdered every night.

"And your name came up."

I put the knife and fork down, and picked up my drink. I took a bracing shot of the stuff. "Who's the stiff?" I asked.

I regretted my choice of words, and somehow knew the name before it left his mouth. "Viva Jasmine."

"Shit."

I wondered if I got her killed, just by talking to her for a while. My sympathy evaporated in the next moment, since I thought myself now to be in the crosshairs somehow. "How am I involved?"

"It's complicated," he said.

"What isn't?"

"Preliminary report says she died of vagal inhibition. Someone who knows their pressure points very well killed her. He did it quick and clean."

"I met with her earlier today," I said. "So when you examined her, it would make sense for me to be in her memory bank."

"There's nothing in her memory bank," he said, and stood over me glowering. "It's empty."

Now I was confused. "So, did she say my name before she died or … Where'd you find her, for starters?"

"In her apartment." Lieutenant Dear massaged the back of his neck. "I slept in a goddamn flop cube on a stakeout last night."

"Neighbor call or something?" I didn't see how someone might overhear a scuffle if whoever killed her had done it quickly and quietly.

"No, the killer called. He's taunting us. He sent a message to SPD and then jetted from the crime scene."

"What did he say?" My stomach lurched. I pushed my plate away from me. I was no longer in the mood to eat.

"His exact words were 'I hail from Tmu Tarakan. I have brought pain and will bring more.'"

"Tmu…" I paused, checked my GenEd mod. All I got was a medieval Russian trading center. I brought up a map on my Enhanced Reality for a moment.

"We were lucky to have one of Timofev's street slingers in lockup today. His rusky buddies know all the tales of the Old Country."

"That's good," I said, killing my ER and causing the map to dissolve before my eyes. "All I'm getting is a literal location of a place that hasn't existed for about a thousand years."

"You got your Babel on?"

"Always," I said, and thought the name *Tmu Tarakan* again. I spoke the two options my mod was giving me. "I've got 'Kingdom of Cockroaches' and 'Place of Darkness.'"

Dear nodded. "Take your pick." He sat back down, after doing a couple more neck rolls. "It's sort of their way of saying East Bumfuck, Egypt. The sticks, the boonies, the middle of nowhere." His eyes grew dark. "It's also like hell, though."

I polished off my drink. The cowpoke came back from the kitchen, smiling widely. He looked down at Dear, sensing something was up. "Can I get you anything, sir?"

"Coffee, thank you."

"Coming right up."

We waited until the server was gone. I leaned forward. "We still haven't gotten to the most important part."

"What?" He asked, blanking before honing in on it. He looked tired. "Oh, your name and how it came up."

"Bingo."

"He used your voice," Dear said. "The killer called us using a rip of your voice he recorded somewhere."

It felt like there was a nest of moths flitting in my stomach and chest. I'd be packing something heavier than the peashooter when I went out this morning. I was relieved at least that Dear was willing to give his old partner the benefit of the doubt, and recognized the voice was a spoof and not me.

He spoke in a register just above whisper. "Johnny, I'm leveling with you. I'm putting my balls in a sling, and my promotion on the line by just coming to you during an open investigation."

"I appreciate it," I said, which was true. I liked to keep tabs on how many killers were watching me at a given time. Between our friend from the Land of Cockroaches and Timofev the current count was two, but there was still time for the number to climb.

"Why were you talking to Viva?"

"She's a friend of a missing person I'm trying to locate." I wasn't going to tell him I knew where Kyra Boxer was. Once SPD got a look at that bite on her chest, they would take her to the hospital and there was no telling if she might wake up and activate her hemlock mod without warning. On top of that, I had the feeling that I still needed Tia Mifune's help and I didn't want to alienate her by betraying her trust.

"What's the name of the person you're looking for?"

"Kyra Boxer," I said.

The cowboy came back out, walking slowly with a chipped porcelain cup filled with sloshing coffee in his hand. "Cream or sugar?"

"Black as my ex-wife's soul."

The server laughed at that and set the mug on a coaster that featured wooly bison stampeding across the plains. "Who is she?" Dear asked me, nodding his "thank you" to the server who departed again.

I pressed the "pay" button on the underside of the unvarnished wooden table and a cylindrical receiver appeared. I wiped my hands so I wouldn't get grease on my sticker. Then I clicked dark coin and a quarter credit into the box, which disappeared upon being paid with the speed of a bank teller's tube.

"Kyra Boxer and Viva Jasmine were into ABDL, playing mommy for rich guys. Doing the diaper thing, the whole nine."

He shook his head. "Whatever floats your boat, I guess. I'm a meat and potatoes guy when it comes to sex." He took a sip of his coffee. "Viva tell you the name of any of her clients?"

"I tried," I said. "She wouldn't divulge."

"I understand." Dear nodded. "Those guys can be susceptible to blackmail if this kind of thing gets out. No one who makes eight figures wants people knowing he can't get his rocks off without a rubber ducky in his bubble bath and a freshly-powdered ass."

I felt a little stab of guilt for not telling him off the record that Bernard Blankstone had been one of Kyra Boxer's clients. But I couldn't explain that without tipping my hand. I was pretty sure he would have someone shadowing me from time to time from here on out in the investigation, regardless of our past friendship or even if he still trusted me. It was nothing personal.

He stood, and I was relieved. I didn't mind his company in general, but I needed some alone time. "Sorry about disturbing your meal," he said.

I shook my head. "It's alright. I can't eat anymore, anyway." That was the truth. Whatever appetite I'd had was killed dead now. I stood with him and we headed for the batwing doors of the saloon.

"Y'all come back now, ya hear?"

Dear flinched from the cliché lobbed at our backsides, and we walked onto the casino floor. The peacock-patterned carpet caught light from the numberless glowing baubles in the chandeliers above us. "I don't mind visiting the Casino Node, but I couldn't live here."

"You get used to it." We weren't heading for the exit, so I assumed he'd come in a department bird on the roof. No more maglev now that he had those gold bars.

He pressed the "up" button on the elevator. "You hear what happened in the Green Node a little while back?"

My heart stutter-stepped. I couldn't tell if we had just waded into a forest of coincidences or if he was playing mind games, if he knew what I knew but was just waiting to goad or guilt me into acknowledging it. "The Grand Poobah himself and one of his Cyborg Yeltsins land in the middle of Kunstler Park, do a quick extraction, and then they ghost."

90

"Who were they extracting?" Now I was playing games with him.

"No clue," he said, either oblivious or playing along. "But before they go, they knock some unicyclist into next Sunday."

"Sounds uncalled for," I said. The elevator came, and Dear stepped on. I stayed put.

"You're not coming?" he asked. "You look like shit. You should get some rest."

"I will," I said. "I've got to take a leak first."

"Alright." The golden doors were closing and he struggled to speak as they shut. "We'll be in touch. Stay safe."

"You too," I said, but the doors were already closed.

A gambler with a polyester Hawaiian shirt and a waddle of fat beneath his chin approached me. I could see he had three synth limbs from some previous sandbox conflict that had probably provided him with a pension large enough to keep him gaming, and keep the anti-trauma drugs pumping from his medical implant twenty-four seven. He had a scorpion bowl filled with sloshing blue alcohol in his hands. The drink smelled like window cleaner so pungent it made the parasol fixed in the liquid wilt like a hothouse flower.

I wasn't general security, but I was still technically an employee of the Zhakpot. "Sir, you can't walk the lobby with that drink. You have to go back to the gaming floor."

"Too late," he said, and poured the contents of the bowl into his mouth as if it was broth and he was starving. Bits of sweet blue mixed drink spilled from the corners of his mouth. "Shit's falling apart."

"What do you mean?"

"Check your scream feeds," he said. "A man's got to stay drunk to deal with these kind of live updates." He walked around me, and I was too curious to collar him and hold him for staff due to his violation of the house rules. Also I didn't want to bust the balls of a vet who'd lost three limbs in some fiery fanatical shithole half a world away.

I streamed into the news feeds and got updates as I headed toward the elevator. I guessed that enough time had elapsed for Dear to assume I had actually been taking a piss if we ran into each other again tonight.

The distressed voice of a female news anchor came through my head. I admired the way she tried to remain professional as she read, even though she probably had quite a stake in the horror she was expected to dispassionately relay. "Green Node Watersheds One and Three are overflowing with non-potable water. Experts believe this has happened due to repeated and successful direct denial of service attacks of a kind previously believed to be firewalled."

It looked like the experts had been wrong again. Maybe I shouldn't have been so hard on them. Defense was harder than offense. Nothing like this had happened in years. I pressed the "up" button on the elevator and waited for the car to come. "Backup reserves are still clean thankfully, but will be used only for essential needs. All fountains and parks will be closed until further notice."

The golden doors opened for me and I stepped inside the elevator. "Shit," I said. I massaged my temples. My heart was still aching for Viva Jasmine. I had no insight into the afterlife. I hoped it consisted of nothing but radiant opium dreams for her in the company of a jade-scaled dragon she could ride in torpid pleasure forever.

Maybe it was a lie but it eased my mind a little, at least until I tuned back into the scream feed. "Footprint calculation algorithms are offline for the whole Schengen. To protect accounts, there will be no energy credit trading until the problem is resolved. Those who want to preserve their balances are invited to keep backup records for their sticks in working order. Resumption of service pending…"

Now things were getting serious. She was no longer speaking like a newscaster. At this point she was sounding like an SOS, reduced at the tail end of what I'd just heard to sentence fragments. I had listened to her casts before, although the anchor's name escaped me and this was the first time her voice had sounded so panic-stricken.

The doors to the elevator opened and I got off. I walked toward my suite, still listening to the news in my head. I switched from audio to an ER version of the cast. I knew my way to my room well enough to navigate there with my enhanced reality output masking my view. I gazed at the anchoress. She had warm brown eyes and sensuous bow-shaped lips.

I pressed my thumbprint over my door, waited for green, and then stepped inside. A light steam rose from Denholm. This was the last stage in his self-cleaning, which was good. I had a couple of assignments for him whenever he finished maintenance on himself. I shed my shoes as easily as a snake dispensing its skin, and I walked to the bed. I plopped down on the mattress that was already shaped to my contours. The bed received me as if I was about to be interred rather than getting ready to sleep for five hours or so.

The news crawl before my eyes continued below the sexy anchor. "Please shield children from energy consumption displays. 'Conservation is contagious' crawls have now been altered to 'Conservation is for cunts.'" I laughed. I was glad that no one was around to see how I could enjoy the crassness, especially when things were so serious. My only alibi was that I was stressed to the breaking point and I needed the relief laughter provided.

"Also ratings should not be heeded," the feed continued. "Many residents of platinum co-ops are reporting their buildings as being labelled condemned."

The news crawl was broken by a gibberish mishmash of hashtags, dollar signs, and an asterisk or two. The caps lock statement "CONSERVATION IS FOR CUNTS" flashed over and over again. This contrasted with the demeanor of the anchoress, who was unaware of what was written below her. It was too much for me to bear, and I turned my ER off. My eyes adjusted to reality or the closest thing to it as the enhancement waned.

Dinner and the drink had been good, the rest of the night a wash. "Cycle complete," Denholm said.

"I'm happy to hear that, my friend."

"Sir, it would appear that quite a bit happened while I was in self-cleaning mode."

"You are correct." I sat up on my elbows, reached behind my head for a pillow, and bunched it behind my neck. "Denholm, can you check the City History and tell me if there's ever been a Schengen-wide spoof before?"

"Yes sir."

Things occasionally went haywire in a node or two, but to the best of my knowledge nothing this extensive had ever been accomplished. "Sir, there are roughly three-hundred thousand attempted attacks on everything from water, photovoltaic, and wind-powered systems per day. There are also an estimated four million spoof attempts per hour, and yet nothing this extensive or destructive has ever happened in the Schengen before."

"I thought so."

I wouldn't be surprised if some of our financial overlords, environmentally-conscious friends, and teenagers plugged deeply into the virtual grid coped with the loss of what they knew as the world by flinging themselves from green rooftops into the mouths of rivers and satellite dishes.

Assuming the maglev kept running, quite a few bodies would be pancaked to the tracks in the morning. Limbs would be severed, windshields covered in sprays of arterial blood, and splats of organs would explode under the pressure of oncoming trains.

"Denholm?"

"Yes sir?"

I stood as quickly as I could, shooting up so that I could deny myself the sleep to which I couldn't surrender before everything that needed doing was done. "I need you to clean my P-90 and load her with crowd dispersal rounds."

"Yes sir."

I walked into the bathroom and splashed water on my face. If there was anarchy in the streets in the morning, I wanted to be ready. I didn't have a desire to body any masked ornery teenage anarchists. I'd mete out some welts and bruises though if anyone tried to get between me and Tia Mifune. I always kept my appointments.

"Have a full canister of spray skin ready, too," I said, and walked over to the Turkish towel on the rack. I dried my face. It was more than possible that I might also get a few bumps and bruises, or that Tia might get scraped or slashed. She struck me as an independent, fierce woman who wouldn't let something like martial law keep her from leaving the fortification of the Ming. She might need some of that antiseptic gel to close wounds. The reverse side of the canister featured an auto-suture gun, which could staple-stitch if it came to that.

I wrapped the towel around my neck and gripped the terrycloth ends as I walked back over to the bed. "Check and see if any birds are available," I said. It was possible that whoever was wreaking havoc on Schengen City might be able to down aircraft as well, but I figured that flying could keep me out of the path of most of any kind of unrest that might erupt tomorrow.

"The Cormorant is available, sir."

"Put a twenty-four hour hold on it," I said. That was a good bird. It had high lift wings, and it could cloak to whatever color the sky was on any given day. The cockpit was also lodged in a nacelle that was a tough nut to crack. It could sustain a direct hit from most anything surface-to-air. If I did get knocked out of the sky or my instrument panel died, I would still stand a good chance of living through the fall. I'd make sure to steer clear of the Edge in any event. If I got knocked out of the sky I wanted it to happen somewhere that I wouldn't risk having the skin picked off my bones after I got grounded.

"Anything else, sir?"

"Yes," I said. "Wind chimes, whale songs, and sea surf until four a.m. Then hit me with an alarm."

"Which alarm, sir? Air horn, call to prayer, rooster crow? Those are the only internal audios I have right now, and it is not advisable to go online and download more at present. The chance of acquiring a virus is very high due to irregularities occurring throughout the various Schengen systems."

"Surprise me," I said. "Lights out." The room grew dark. "Milky Way." A pallid and mysterious swirl of a galaxy enveloped the room in its uncanny light, washing over me like interstellar amniotic fluid.

"Goodnight, Denholm."

"Goodnight, sir," my best friend said.

CHAPTER TWELVE

UNCANNY ENCOUNTER

Havoc was still coursing through the Schengen as I got in the bird. The latest bit I caught from the scream feeds before unplugging had to do with an automated synth-beef cutting machine going haywire and slicing off a soy butcher's right hand.

I figured that the Ming wouldn't be playing around, so I subvoc'd a command to the Cormorant. "Activate Sky Grab."

"Activated," a calm female voice said.

Any surface-to-air defenses the Ming had against unidentified craft would hopefully not be triggered, and no sensor alarms would go off when I touched down on the roof. "Undercarriage cameras," I said. I got a view of Chinatown beneath me, a parade centered around a red paper dragon snaking through the streets and bringing traffic to a standstill. Fireworks sparkled and popped around the crimson monster.

I entered the luxury building's radar zone without getting any warnings on my glowing instrument panel. So far, so good. The sun made me squint hard enough to activate the tint bubble, which drew over the craft like myelin over a brain. The previously gemstone-colored skin of the Ming was dyed copper by the sun's rays and the whole city shined like something minted in a goldsmith's dream.

The rooftop appeared beneath me. There was a gathering of aerodyne landing pads, microwave dishes, and the odd photovoltaic panel. I avoided the one grid square of the roof that was a skylight, and I touched down.

"Hover," I said to the craft as I got out. My senses were on high alert, and I wanted to be able to bugout quick if something wasn't right below. I wasn't sure if Tia Mifune was involved in what I thought was a blackmail scheme gone awry. I had told her I would be here this morning, but I didn't want to tell her the exact time or announce my presence by paging her on the platinum com box below.

I walked to the door on the roof, leading into the building. "Spoof Mifune, Tia." I felt a woman's voice vibrating in my larynx, and I spoke in the dulcet tone of the Touch CEO. "Please let me in."

The red clicked green and I walked inside. The walls of the stairwell shined a sickly color from the force of mercury vapor lamps lighting the passageway. I reached the landing where Tia Mifune lived, opened the door, and walked down the hall toward her apartment.

I was subvoc'ing from here on out, as I didn't want to tip my hand before going inside. I looked once left and right, before speaking to Denholm. "I need my eyes," I said, and the contact lens enhancement relay I kept in his head started to work.

"Yes, sir." Maybe it was my imagination, but he sounded revived. That was probably owing to his recent self-cleaning. "Starlight activated," my English friend said in my head. "Auto-tuning to account for light conditions in the apartment."

"Take your time." I reflexively touched the gun and the medical spray hidden underneath my jacket with both my hands. My right leg was a bit game since I'd been putting off a visit to the doctor to check an old ACL tear I got while on meat beat. If I had to break down the door to the apartment, I'd be using my recently-checked cybered arm. This was assuming that the door had somehow already been spoofed to remain locked when I tried to trick it open.

"Reading complete," Denholm said.

"Transfer to ER view." The enhanced reality mod allowed me to see through the wall into the apartment. Two forms were lying on the floor in the room farthest from the entrance, splayed out with weak signatures. That meant they were either dead, in the process of dying, or they were surrounded by beds of ice. I didn't think they were building snowmen while I was gone.

My eyes honed in on something smaller and nearer, an oval-shaped signature of pulsing heat no larger than a Faberge egg. "Sir, this object has not yet been identified. The other two are Tia Mifune and Kyra Boxer. Both are deceased."

I pulled my gun out of my jacket and held it in my right hand. "Find out what the hell that thing is," I said, of the egg.

"Yes sir."

"Image acquired."

"Model it on a 3D wireframe and then give me a three-sixty."

"Yes sir."

My palm was sweating on the crosshatched polymer grip of my piece. "Motherfucker." All three of my main contacts on this case were dead. I had shit for leads, and besides that I wasn't callous enough not to feel bad for failing to protect anyone. Chivalry might have gone the way of the dodo and the panda, but I still had a little bit of it left in me and I had screwed up royally.

"Image completed, sir."

"Screen on ER."

It appeared before me, shaped more like an almond than an egg in this perspective. "Bring up the menu at Saki Tumi," I said.

"Working, sir…"

A list of items from a traditional Korean joint fought with space on my ER app, against the rotating thing that bore an uncanny resemblance to a golden-fried… "Beondegi!" I subvoc'd, finally latching onto the image. I had meant my subvoc'd thought as a personal *Eureka!* moment, but Denholm had taken it as a literal command. That was all for the best, since the image he brought up when contrasted with the thing in the apartment only made the comparison more apt.

I doubted that whatever we were dealing with was a golden-fried silkworm pupa however much it looked like one. An idea suddenly occurred to me. My brainstorm was either inspired, stupid, or some combination of the two. We would soon find out.

I kept the piece in my right hand, but reached inside my jacket with the left and pulled out the spray-on skin. "Oscillate Tia Mifune through the larynx again."

"Go ahead, sir."

"I'm home," I said, and the door sprung inward. I rushed toward the brown egg, whose leathery skin started to peel open like a Venus flytrap sensing nearby prey. My skin crawled as I saw the slimy hide curl outward. It left a film that broke and bled like a female hymen upon being punctured. Whatever was inside the egg and wanted out wasn't getting its chance today. I sprayed the skin onto the opening egg, which contracted and froze in confusion.

I depressed the trigger of the spray nozzle until the oval was suffused in white foam that hardened around the cockroach-colored beondegi. The egg was sticky and grafted to the floor of the apartment, cemented in place by its own secretions and my chemical compliment. I let the empty aerosol can drop to the floor.

"May I ask what you're doing, sir?"

"Are you curious?" I asked Denholm.

"I don't know if you would define it as that, sir. I am programmed to study your actions. When one does not accord with any previous action, I am supposed to collect new data to better serve you."

"I see."

"The medical skin spray is meant to heal wounds, is it not?"

"Yes," I said, "but it also has properties that can seal. There are cheaper ways to caulk holes in the walls of your apartment, though."

"It is expensive, sir," Denholm allowed. "The price has gone up by two dark coin since you last purchased a bottle. Would you like me to purchase another one now?"

"Yes," I said, and walked slowly toward where the faint signatures the women radiated. I didn't need a coroner to pronounce time of death. I could get that from Denholm.

"Is that all you needed to know about the skin?" I asked. "If I needed more?"

"No sir. Why did you use it on that beondegi?"

I could smell the bedroom as I walked toward it. The room reeked of patchouli oil and incense burning in a sandalwood holder. The door to the bedroom was closed. I still spoke subvoc, just in case the killer was behind the door I was headed toward. "Check all asymmetrical warfare and counter-terrorism pamphlets. Do a review and get back to me."

"I will, sir."

"That egg thing looked natural, but our resourceful craftsman knows how to combine and splice the organic and the mechanical. I think that thing is a bouncing Betty of some kind. Were I to shoot it as whoever set the booby-trap intended, it might have exploded and discharged ordinance or something worse." I thought about the tongue with the eyes and mouth of its own that had flashed in Bernard Blankstone's head before his skull exploded. I shuddered for what must have been the tenth time that day.

"Very good, sir."

"Here goes nothing." I kept the gun in my right hand and battered the door down with my cybered arm.

Both Tia Mifune and Kyra Boxer were naked on the bed set in the bamboo frame. A soft light glowed from an incense holder shaped like a serene Buddha meditating with downcast eyes. A stick of Nag Champa was smoldering in there. I moved my eyes and my gun in time together around the room.

I walked toward the two women entwined on the bed. A coat of blood thick as finger paint covered the women, red gashes the size of open mouths puckering all over their pale forms. Kyra Boxer's right breast, previously swollen and infected, was no more. It had been torn free and now there was a red-ringed hollow where a handful of flesh had been scooped out. I guessed that was where the mod had been, and whoever had put it in now wanted his hardware back.

Aside from the gore, there was also a trickling drizzle of blood that led away from the bed. The trail ended by the dim sum bowl, where a d-cup breast that drooped too naturally to be an implant swam in a red bath. The fatty tissue of the breast combined with the heat of the water in the porcelain cup to give off a smell sickeningly similar to that of chicken broth.

"Okay," I said. I wasn't a rookie but I had come across too much, too fast.

"Sir," Denholm said, barely audible over the sound of my retching. I vomited onto the shiatsu stones arrayed at my feet.

I wiped chunks of vomitus from my lips. "What?"

"Look on the wall just above you, sir."

I'd forgotten that he was still running in the background programs, since I hadn't told him to go to sleep. Written in streaking letters in blood on the white wall was "Tmu Tarakan."

"I know what it means," I said.

"I know you have a GenEd mod, sir."

I spit a final string of vomit and snarled at him, "I know what it means to the Russkies, too." I didn't mean to be curt with him, but I was under pressure. I shifted the gun from right to cybered hand so that I could wipe the sweat from my palm onto my slacks.

"I'm aware you know the folkloric meaning of the phrase too, sir. I ran over your conversation with Lieutenant Dear in the Goldmine last night."

I couldn't fault him for that. If this thing ever went to trial, I would need all the minutes, recordings, and notes I had accumulated. I had all of that internally, but it never hurt to have a backup.

"Sir, I was pointing out the message on the wall for another reason."

"Which is?"

"It's been done in your handwriting."

I looked up to confirm. I had never bothered to write in such large letters, even when practicing cursive like the cyber docs suggested. There was no mistaking my flourishes, curlicues, and general MD-worthy sloppiness. "Shit."

This was bad. I was the first on a crime scene with two dead women, one of whose location I had omitted knowing last night while talking to a ranking officer about an ongoing investigation. My DNA was on the floor in the form of vomit and bile, and now a message written in my hand was scrawled in the blood of two mutilated women.

I was being framed, but I might have a hard time convincing the SPD of that even though I had friends there. My friends weren't as powerful as Bernard Blankstone's and if I could be traced to his murder, I'd be sharing cells with people I'd put away. It was true I had put them away a long time ago, but they had good memories and nothing but time on their hands. We all had goals in life, and one of mine was to avoid that permanent barcode tat that would mark me as a felon.

I had two options now. I could either stay here and call SPD and have them take me down to the station and try to acquit myself, or I could get the hell out of here with that frozen egg. This was assuming it hadn't thawed and its payload wouldn't head for me soon. SPD would eventually catch up to me, but maybe I would have enough time to give Timofev a name. All I would ask in return from the kingpin would be for him to put out a pass for me to do easy time in lockup, until either my name got cleared or I ended up serving for multiple murder beefs.

"Okay, Denholm. I'm ghosting. This is enough fun for one day."

"Probably a good idea, sir."

"Keep all programs running in the background. Let me know if Dear or any of his boys are on my ass."

"Sir, something is already 'on your ass' as you say."

My adrenaline pumped. "Who, where?"

"Behind you."

I turned, and a baby on all fours started crawling toward me. "Baby want milk. Baby want mommy."

I backed up so hard that I tripped and fell to the ground, bruising my right palm and accidentally punching through the hardwood floor beneath me as I landed with the full force of my cybered arm. The hole I'd smashed into the floor gave view onto a woman bathing in a claw-footed tub with a steamed towel lain over her face. She pulled the cloth from her eyes and shrieked.

"Mommy, baby want titty! Baby want milky! Feed Bernie Baby!"

I knew it wasn't real. The lips didn't move as the looped program played. After the last demand from the baby I knew this was a recording of Bernard Blankstone's voice.

The vinyl doll was so realistic that I could see the hairs on its head, as silky as those of a duck's behind. I didn't even have to squint to see the blue veins tracing beneath the pale skin. The infant boy bot wore a blue organza bow on its head. Its legs and face were robust with baby fat. It would have been quite a cute cherub, if it didn't have designs of killing me or perhaps exploding onto me when I took a shot at it.

I didn't have a choice this time, as I was out of spray skin. "Baby Bernard want booby!" I squeezed the trigger on my piece and there was a flash. A hole the size of a poker chip appeared in the baby's porcelain skin. The metal, PVC, and wired inner workings of the baby's head revealed themselves. A laser flash waved toward me and I ducked. A succession of hollow point rounds ripped the far wall of the room. I rolled right and briefly contemplated pistol-whipping the infant's remnants. Instead I brought the fist of my left arm down hard on what remained of his head so that it shattered and the polymer casing of the gun beneath the baby doll's head broke into component parts as well.

A mixture of emotions washed over me, all of them ugly. I hadn't killed a kid, but the thing was too lifelike for my senses to fully know that. I had seen, arrested, and killed my fair share of sick human beings. I was convinced that none of them was as sick as whoever was behind this. Whoever they were, they were smarter than anyone I'd tussled with before, which just made me more afraid.

This was the first time I found myself thinking I might lose in a war of wits with a criminal. And it wasn't just the layoff and the years spent doing house dick work at the Zhakpot and letting my skills rust and my faculties collect mothballs. I doubted that I could have beaten whoever I was now up against now back when I was in my prime, before I'd gotten hurt.

Still I had no choice but to keep going. I technically had no client, but I was curious and enraged. That was more than enough to fuel me.

The shrieks of the woman on the floor below me brought me out of my thoughts, and the single-shot she fired from her anti-intruder polymer also put my troubles into perspective. The round hit the outside of my clamshell jacket, sparks danced, and the brass jacket of the round fell back through the hole I'd punched in the floor. The casing landed on the woman's arm.

"Ow!" She grabbed the part of her forearm that burned, and dropped the gun to the tile floor of her bathroom where water heavy with bubbles overflowed from the tub. I didn't blame her for shooting at me, although if she'd fired a bit further north I might have currently had a pretty bad headache.

I ran through the apartment, snagged the egg in my fake arm in case it was contaminated or poisonous on contact with real skin, and then I rushed through the front door. I bowled over two concerned neighbors who stood in the hallway. My panic was so intense that I didn't have time to feel bad about flooring one and sending the other into the far wall of the corridor hard enough to chip plaster. I was running so fast when I hit them that I couldn't give a description of either, not even their sex. I knew nothing except enough to tell by feel that they were made of meat and not heavily modded. Those two plus the woman below gave me a tally of three hurt civilians, in addition to three other people who'd been breathing before they made my acquaintance.

I thought as I rushed for the Cormorant on the roof that maybe I didn't have what it took to do this job anymore. I thought maybe I should stick to pilfered towels and stolen complimentary chocolate mints at the Zhakpot Hotel.

CHAPTER THIRTEEN

BACK TO THE WONDER CHAMBER

The killer had obviously gotten a sample of my handwriting on the night I'd left a message for Viva Jasmine with Russel Nadler. I hoped that Nadler had only allowed my info to be compromised by accident, but anything was possible. Detective Dear had given me the benefit of the doubt when someone had spoofed my voice to call SPD, but finding my writing in blood on the wall in a room where dead women lay might be too much to swallow.

I steered the Cormorant around behind the Import-Export warehouse adjacent to Lazlo's shop, wondering how long it was going to be before I was picked up for murder.

It was unload time at the service dock in the rear of the building, and I touched down and deployed landing plates while two fixed wing cargo vessels cooled their jets. Their bays yawned open, and Chinese workers in blue chino jumpsuits rushed out of the warehouse toward the new delivery.

Someone dropped a packing crate, and concrete paving bricks used for Taekwondo spilled out onto the ground. One of the workers whispered something in Mandarin and quickly hustled the block back into the bed of straw. It was safe to assume that delivering a hard knife-hand strike to one of those blocks would reveal smuggled opium tar or hashish bricks.

I was burdened with my own secrets to keep, and I held the strange frozen egg in my left hand. I figured that if the skin of one of my hands was going to be peeled off, it should be the one that didn't feel pain. The left could be dismounted and re-grafted in the time it took to read the scream feeds on my ER mod.

I found that Lazlo had another toy hooked up upon entrance to his Wonder Chamber. I pushed the door open with my right hand, and was treated to a view of a submarine made from a potbelly stove. The sub's cast iron door served as a vivisected view onto two seamen at work. One was wearing a sailor's scrambled eggs cap and manning the torpedoes. His friend was dressed like a longshoreman, and operated a periscope by pedaling on his bicycle. The only problem was that no portion of the display worked.

"I caught your little friends between performances?" I looked toward the back of the store.

Lazlo pushed back from his bench and floated in his swivel chair to get a better look at the intruder. He was wearing a half-mask respirator with raccoon-eyed goggles for protection. His face was covered in bioluminescent bacteria. "Get your ass back here!" His voice was muffled, and he pulled the mask off to better chastise me.

"What did I do?"

He set his paintbrush in a bucket filled with bioluminescence that glowed like a radiant firefly. Before him on his workbench were models of tropical fish made from shaped fragments of corroded metal. He had been applying finishes to their stripes when I came in.

"Let's start with that." He pointed at the egg. "What the hell is that?"

"This," I held it up in my nerveless left hand. "This is a bit of ordinance your genius chemist set up to kill me today."

Lazlo studied it. "Why aren't you dead?"

I shrugged. "Maybe because I'm smarter than this asshole thought."

"Be right back." Lazlo stood up and walked across the room.

"It was getting ready to open up on me, and I flooded it with spray skin. That seemed to seal it right up."

"Yeah," his voice came to me. "That was a smart move, but it ain't gonna be sealed forever."

I heard him rummaging through storage and all his assorted effects. I hoped to god that he wasn't going to bring his stupid duck back out. "Then let's hurry up," I said. "I'm double-parked anyway." I could feel the payload stirring like an incubated chick getting ready to break through its shell and escape out into the world.

Lazlo wheeled a metal sphere toward me. It was coated in tungsten and shined. I didn't know how much it weighed, but I hazarded that not even the man with the strongest cybered arms in the world could deadlift it.

"What is that thing?"

He opened the hatch. "I've been using it as a vacuum cleaner around the shop." He pulled a hose attachment from inside of the berth. Lazlo brought a bag of lint out of the contraption and then motioned for me to toss the egg inside.

I obliged by dropping it in, and then stood back. Lazlo slammed the top shut on his device, and then leaned down to fiddle with an array of knobs and readouts on the far face of the metal ball. I crouched down on the other side and asked, "So aside from being a vacuum cleaner, what else can this thing do?"

"It's a BCV Eurozone Conflict Blast Containment Vessel."

"Bomb disposal?" I'd gotten my stripes in the force, but I'd missed out on any one of our numberless sandbox engagements abroad.

"Exactly. You can set it for primary and secondary detonations, and get analysis readouts on whatever's in the bomb once she's blown. If you said it was ready to open before you froze it with the spray skin, then I say we just set this thing's thermals to room temperature and see what happens when we thaw her."

He stood back and I followed suit. "It'll take a minute," he said, and walked over to an industrial sink with two baths. He took off his gloves and set them in one side of the sink, and then turned the water on. This was the first time I'd seen him without his regular getup of goggles and top hat.

I walked back over to the bucket filled with paint. "It's pretty, but this stuff makes a mess."

He dunked his head under the faucet and ran cold water over his neck. "It leaves a trail, too. You got to be careful when you're draining it from the trees. You don't want the cops following you."

I shook my head. "You siphoned that?"

He giggled. "Yeah, from Loomoo Park. Shit's too expensive to pay for out of pocket." He wagged his head from side to side like a dog, and then looked toward the beaded gypsy curtain separating the workshop from the store. "You see my submarine out there?"

"Yeah, it ain't working."

His face turned scarlet with rage. I had never seen him angry before. "No more kids in the shop. I tried to be cool, but that's it."

"Some kid break your toy?"

Lazlo's anger shifted a bit to me. "It's not a toy. It's a model."

"Okay, same question, different noun."

He shook his head. "This generation can solve any equation for 'x' before they lose their baby teeth, but tell them to turn something clockwise and watch four months' worth of work go down the drain."

I decided to let the subject drop. Lazlo walked back over to the metal orb and studied the panel on the side like a baker checking to see if his bread was done. "Still needs a couple more minutes." He leaned on the side of the ball, which I didn't think was advisable no matter how armored the thing was.

He eyed me gravely. "Johnny, we got fucking beacoup problems my man." He licked his vampire fangs.

"I got too many problems to count, Lazlo. You got to be more specific."

"I'm not saying any names."

"Okay," I said. That sounded reasonable enough. He apparently didn't like the idea of skydiving without a parachute any more than I did.

"A certain Asian gentleman and his friends in this neighborhood say there's a Russian-Kazak who's crawling around here, following *your* trail..." He pointed to me. "His goons are poking around *my* store." He jabbed a thumb into his chest for emphasis.

I pulled my sticker from my clamshell without further delay. "No one is saying you won't be compensated." I waited for him to show me his own currency wand, but he surprised me by rolling up his sleeve and showing me a barcode waver on the underside of his right wrist.

Those mods were never my style, probably because I'd seen prisoners using them to buy commissary snacks whenever my trips downtown took me to the Schengen Dungeon. If he occasionally wanted to get paid through the skin that was his affair. I clicked a solid number of dark coin, and laced that with credits like a dash of wasabi on sushi.

He calmed a bit. Now that I'd paid him, I decided to guilt him a little too. "I know you admire this guy's skill, but he just killed three women. You don't get any relief, I don't get any relief, and neither of our powerful friends gets any relief until our boy is found. Be they Kazak or Chinese, they don't breathe easy until this case is wrapped with a pretty bow on top. You follow me?"

"Yeah." He averted his eyes. "You're right. This guy's fucking everyone's system up. You been watching scream feeds?"

"Yes I have. Remind me to stay away from automated butchers for a while."

The metal globe dinged, and Lazlo walked back over to it. He looked at me. "Bring up your ER," he said. I did.

"Internal view," Lazlo said. We got a live feed from the micro-cameras inside of the walls of the vessel. They had deployed from behind shield plates once it was determined the explosion either hadn't happened or had passed, and it was now safe for the cameras to come out for a peek.

The skin of the egg had not only dried from where I had softened it with the medical skin, but it was as flaky as a maple leaf in late autumn. Rather than breaking it unwound like a spooled bobbin covered in silk. A spider the size of a man's hand jumped out.

"Jesus," I said. Its eight legs were the color of frozen amber, covered in mottled yellow and brown semitransparent skin like the frames of tortoiseshell glasses. The limbs were shaggy as pipe cleaners and covered in black fur. The body on which the legs sat like stilts was particolored, looking like a ripe tropical poisonous strawberry.

"Denholm," I subvoc'd.

"What?" Lazlo said. I didn't know his system was on. It was probably always activated, although that wasn't recommended. Leaving a subvoc implant running twenty-four seven was unhealthy for reasons the cyber psychotherapists never deduced, although the scientists knew enough to know it caused a condition that mimicked schizophrenia.

"Yes sir?"

"I need your eyes."

"Yes sir."

My butler used the contact lens I'd installed in his eye to gaze through the metal and study the cocoon from which the spider unwound. "It is aciniform silk, sir. Spiders wrap their prey in this."

"Okay."

The spider now diligently used its legs with the dexterousness of opposable thumbs to slice through another small egg that was nested inside of the larger one like a Matryoshka doll.

"What about the spider itself? I'm not getting anything on my GenEd from the images you're giving me."

"It's transgenically modified, sir. It is not totally a spider, although constituents of it come from the golden orb family. The rest of its makeup is synthetic craftsmanship."

"Master craftsmanship," Lazlo said.

I had meant this as a two-way conversation. I had the security to ensure it as such, but I wasn't surprised to hear Lazlo butting in telepathically. "What does it look like is in the egg?" I asked.

"I believe," Denholm said, "that it is a bomb, sir."

The images flashed white in a concussive strobe. Just like a kid when playing one of their videogames, my mirror neurons tricked me into believing for a moment that the remote perspective I enjoyed was my own eyes. I thought for a millisecond that I was dead. I would have been if I hadn't thought on my feet up there in Tia Mifune's apartment.

"Stop talking to the English chap," Lazlo ordered.

"Denholm," I said, "Background."

"Yes sir, although I believe you said you wanted me to bone up on asymmetrical warfare and explosive ordinance disposal."

"Sure," I said. "Just don't burn the candle at both ends."

He paused to run through idioms until he found the "Candle" section. Then he replied, "Very good sir."

Lazlo continued studying, interpreting the readout on his giant titanium orb while speaking to me. "I've got to get one of those. How much was he?"

I knew Denholm was only a machine, but it didn't feel right talking about him as if he was chattel. "He was gifted to me by the Zhakpot. I modded him out." That meant I thought a piece of my soul was in the old Englishman.

"Okay," Lazlo said. "I don't know what these particles are floating around in the bomb the spider was guarding. I can tell you though that four of them would be toxic enough to kill something the size of a rhesus monkey."

"How many are in there?" I wasn't sure I wanted to know.

"Five-thousand," Lazlo said. He looked up at me with fear in his eyes. "It's not enough to kill everyone in the Schengen, but it probably would be enough to cause casualties in the thousands. The node where the egg opened would get locked down on quarantine until Eurozone Health Authorities gave the all clear, which could take weeks. This thing could have ruined everyone's weekend at the very least. I'll kill all germs inside via sterilization cycle after I run some more tests. And I'll make sure to kill the spider, too."

"So what are we dealing with here?" I asked.

Lazlo turned his device around and wheeled it back toward the rear of the workshop. "We're dealing with someone who's either going to get caught and killed soon, or who's going to probably keep fucking around and making bigger plans until it's probably bye-bye Schengen."

I hollered toward Lazlo as he replaced his bomb destroyer somewhere in storage. "Did you pick up anything else?"

"Yeah, but nothing toxic or dangerous."

"What was it?"

He squinted, confused by his own discovery. "Casein, it's a milk protein." He scratched his head. "It's mammalian. I've got no idea what the hell it's doing in a spider."

"You find out anything from that hypo I left here?" I pointed toward the bench where he'd set the needle the last time we'd met.

"Yeah, but Ivan the Terrible's goons came in and jacked it from me before I could run any more tests." He pointed toward the metal container he'd just rolled to the back of the shop. "I'm going to run some more tests on the stuff in that vessel, but I don't want it laying around just in case the Russkies or the Chinamen try to confiscate it for their own purposes."

"Yeah, I wouldn't use it as a vacuum cleaner for a day or two either."

He wasn't in the mood to laugh. "If the Triad and the Russian mob get into a crosstown beef, it could get ugly." He held up his arms in exasperation. "I'm a tinker, man. I love my shop. I don't want to get caught up in a fucking arms race or a shootout."

I patted him with my right hand, walked over to his sink, and said, "We'll get out of this spider's web. Just give me a few days." I turned on the faucet and stuck my left hand underneath its stream. My left arm's sensors were still off and I couldn't tell if the water was hot or cold. "You got any decontaminate?" I asked

"Yeah, but I wouldn't worry about the skin of that egg thing. The poison was in the payload, not the skin."

"Forget it, then." I turned the sink off, and started toward the front of the shop. The last thing I needed was for the Cormorant to get impounded. I figured it was only a matter of time until the dockworkers behind the Import-Export warehouse got wise and realized I wasn't there to make deliveries, at least not of the nature that they were accustomed to receiving.

"If I hear anything, I'll let you know," Lazlo said to my retreating form.

I broke through the beaded curtain and walked back through the front of the shop, and out into the street. The smell of frying duck made my mouth water. I turned the corner into the alleyway sandwiched between two brick buildings, scaring away an alley cat with jaundiced eyes as I approached. "Don't end up in a wok, little buddy."

Behind the building the workers walked toward the warehouse bay door carrying vitrines filled with various pickled animals and white plastic boxes labeled "Medical Land Acupuncture Needles." I didn't ask questions, and they didn't pay me any mind as I did a beeline for the Cormorant. I unlocked the bird, started its engine, and lifted the landing pads in one quick subvocalized command. I reflexively touched my gun, which was still warm from being fired at that baby thing a little earlier today.

I got into the bird, and Denholm's voice was in my ear. "Sir?"

"Yes sir?" I said.

Throwing the honorific back at him startled him, or at least threw a glitch in his programming matrix. He quickly rebounded. "I made a recording of your entire conversation with Lazlo the Toymaker. I believe you gave me specific instructions to record, transcribe, and keep records of any investigation-related interactions except those that take place between you and any member of Vasily Timofev's organization."

"That's correct. There's nothing to apologize for. I'm sure Lazlo was recording me." I lifted off into the sky, the buildings of Chinatown growing smaller below.

"I'm not calling to apologize, sir. I'm calling to confirm that the casein Lazlo identified in the bomb is sometimes used by Stelios Labs, in the Industrial Zone."

"Go on." I'd flown over the place and driven past its grim Stalinist façade on maglev rides, but I'd never inquired into its business.

"Sir, Stelios is involved in both research and manufacturing using spider silk enhanced by such milk proteins."

I aimed the conical nose of the ship toward the light pollution of the Casino Node on the horizon. The Statue of Liberty, the Sphinx, and Eiffel Tower beckoned. "What do they do research on?"

"Sir, they test the silks for conductivity and antistatic applications. They try to find better ways to provide barriers against electromagnetic interference, both attacks and accidents. They also research radiofrequency anomalies coming from the Edge into the Nodes."

"Sounds like the kind of thing that should be hush-hush," I said. "How are you just accessing this stuff so easily? Someone order food subvocally from a takeout restaurant's website you've been monitoring, you sly devil?"

I veered right to make way for a formation of seeding dirigibles floating through the purple thunderheads. I had yet to check the screamers of late. Things certainly felt calmer, although that could have just been the high vantage I now enjoyed. I hoped the attack was over and that the storm had been weathered.

"Sir, Stelios is a nonprofit founded only for defensive purposes. It also manufactures clothing from spider silk, which is donated to refugees from the Edge."

"I see."

"That is at least their mission statement, sir. Thus you can see why they value transparency, and even welcome visitors on walkthrough tours."

I steered toward the helipad on top of the Zhakpot, and slackened my thrust. The craft drifted downward. "Denholm, are you dropping hints that I should maybe take a fieldtrip?"

"It wouldn't be a bad idea, sir."

I landed, and clicked the button on the instrument panel that let the on-staff mechanic know routine service and maintenance needed to be done.

"You might be right," I said. I unbuckled my seatbelt and stepped out of the craft. I staggered onto the tarmac with rubbery legs. Neon pulsed and flickered over the buildings and streets, bled across my skin in rust red and ice blue.

That spider could have come from anywhere, as could the silk and the casein. But there was a local research lab that had spiders, casein, and silk, all of which had been in the bomb that had been planted to kill me. It wouldn't hurt to check the place out. The milk constituent- the casein- might have linked the spider to the breasts and to the fetish and the implants somehow. The link was tenuous and only in my mind for the moment. That didn't mean I wouldn't be able to put it all together later, especially if Lazlo found out anything else from the bomb remnants he had trapped in that glorified vacuum cleaner of his.

"Shit," I said. The night was humid, my hair was plastered to my forehead, and my mouth was sticky. I needed a drink, but a cold one on the rocks.

"Sir, there's one last bit of information that, according to my records, makes me think Stelios Labs may be of some interest to you."

I walked across the tarmac toward the door on the roof. "Denholm, you've already sold me on this job but what else you got for me?"

"Sir, the nonprofit was founded by Bernard Blankstone. According to the screamer gossip, the project was his favorite among all of his various philanthropic and charitable holdings."

That made me stop in my tracks. "Get the hours," I said. "Make the appointment. Set a subvoc alarm to wake me two hours before they open."

"Yes sir."

I started walking toward the roof door again. "That'll give me time to shower and hit the continental breakfast downstairs."

"Yes sir."

"Oh," I said, grabbing the handle of the rooftop door that led down into the Zhakpot.

"Sir?"

"Actually, two things." The door recognized the whorls of my fingerprints and let me in. I walked down the carpeted hallway.

"Yes sir."

"Make sure to run a bomb sweep of any vehicle I step into from here on out. I'm out of spray skin, and I might not be so lucky next time."

"Yes sir." Denholm paused. "What was the second thing, sir?"

"Stop calling me sir."

He couldn't laugh, but I hoped there was amusement firing in his brainbox circuitry. "Sir, I cannot comply with that order."

"Yeah," I said, "I figured."

CHAPTER FOURTEEN

END OF THE SILK ROAD

Twenty minutes spent pondering the stick figure composed of golden fibers didn't bring me any closer to understanding what it was. The receptionist at Stelios Labs looked up from filing her nails and pointed to the thing shining like Rapunzel's golden locks.

"It's installation art," she said.

"Thank you." I stood and walked around the thing on its pedestal.

"It's composed entirely of golden orb spider silk," she said.

"It is quite impressive," someone else said. The new voice behind me was high and adenoidal. I turned around and saw a man who looked to be having sinus problems, with a snub nose and a smattering of pock scars erupting over his leathery skin. He wore a white lab coat and sported a paisley tie flecked with gold that shined like polyester that I was sure belonged to one of the spiders.

"Welcome to Stelios. I'm Doctor Gennady Anatole."

He extended a skeletal hand and I took it in my grasp. "Thank you for seeing me on such short notice."

"Yes, it is probably a good thing that you maintained your security clearance after retirement from the force. Those things are a devil to reinstate."

He waved the whorls of his pointer finger over a reader and the bolt on a door separating reception from labs clicked open. He turned toward me as we started down a hall with white walls. "Understand, we are open to the public. But it usually takes a week or two to organize a tour. We must be careful about espionage when a project is ongoing, but we are always happy to share our results once the Blankstone Foundation has resolved the matter of rights and patent."

I stopped before a room on the right. An oblong window gave view onto two other technicians, one male and the other female. Both were in lab coats and wearing latex gloves. They looked to be working over a microscope of some kind.

Dr. Anatole stopped with me, and grinned. "Would you like to see what they're doing?"

"Please," I said.

The good doctor waved his finger over the reader on the door to the lab and opened the door for me. "Thank you." I walked in before him, and headed over to the table where the male and female tech labored over a slumbering spider. It looked very much like the one that tried to kill me.

The woman was a redhead with brown eyes. She smiled at me. "I've just hit her with carbon dioxide to relax her."

The woman's partner was a man with curly hair and a flouncing waddle of fat beneath his chin. He taped the spider down to the Teflon-coated plate on which it slept. "I'm holding the banana spider in place, so that silk can be extracted."

Both of their lines sounded well-rehearsed, and I was certain they were used to having their work interrupted like this by tours. "Is there a difference," I asked, "between a golden orb spider and a banana spider?"

"No, no," the man said. "A banana spider is a golden orb spider. I wouldn't use the term in a peer-reviewed journal." He grinned at me. "But we're amongst friends."

Dr. Anatole's voice grew tense. "This makes her tired, but it doesn't hurt her."

"She's happy to do it," the redheaded tech said, her own unassuming smile widening on her face. I wondered how someone could grow so attached to an arachnid. "She got a cricket before this to make her happy."

I thought of something. "Do animal rights activists sometimes give you guys a hard time?"

"They are impossible to please." Doctor Anatole clapped his hands together and sanded them one against the other. "We are obligated by law to provide some form of recreation for any animal we use in tests." He looked up at me. "How pray tell does one provide recreation for a spider?"

"Crickets," the female tech said.

"Then those who love crickets will call us killers." Doctor Anatole massaged his hands against his scalp, moistening the gray strands of his receding hairline into a respectable comb over.

"Let's see how this last mod worked out." The male tech stuffed a tiny set of tweezers into an orifice on the spider too minute for me to see without help from Denholm.

"What are you doing?"

The redhead spoke while her coworker maneuvered the tweezers inside the sleeping spider. "We did a mod on her to make her produce dragline silk at an exponential rate. We want to see if it worked."

The other tech labored with the careful scrutiny of a jeweler. He spoke to me in a voice barely above a whisper, as if he feared the patient might awaken on the Pyrex mount. He pulled the golden thread from the slumbering spider's pouch and fed the end onto a spool on the corner of the tabletop.

"Pull," I heard the scientist using his subvoc mod for the first time that day, commanding the spool to rotate and yank the shimmering thread from the spider.

"Count length," the redheaded tech said. She spoke to me as she subvoc'd, which required more coordination than I had. "She had an original capacity to spin about ninety meters of silk in a session."

"She's on track to spin about a thousand this time," her partner said.

"That's not bad," I said.

"Not bad," he replied. "But not exponential."

The rate of unwinding from the spider slowed, and the spool gathered more silk until it bore an uncanny resemblance to the cocoon that had been shielding the bomblet I'd seen earlier inside the egg. I thought back to Denholm's initial analysis of what he'd seen in that bomb chamber.

"What kind of silk is that?" I pointed at the tiny tightrope balancing between spider and spool.

"It's dragline silk," the redhead said. "It's what spiders use as a lifeline in case they fall."

Doctor Anatole spoke, "It's also what the spiders use to build the frames and spokes of their webs."

"What's its practical purpose?" I asked. "I mean, for humans?"

The spider was tapped out, and no more thread poured from it. The male tech took the single swatch of tape from the spider and lovingly cradled her his hands, carrying her out of the room.

"It can be used as arresting wire with aircraft," the female tech said. She walked over to a trashcan in the corner and hit the foot treadle. She discarded her rubber gloves and walked over to a hand sanitation station and talked as she washed her hands. "Other types are used for more fine work, such as sutures and stitches for ligaments."

Doctor Anatole nodded to her. "Thank you Keri." He looked at me to gauge my level of satisfaction with the display.

I wasn't quite finished yet. "You said 'she.'"

"Yes?" Keri said. Her eyebrow arched, as if she was waiting for me to either sexually impugn her or the spider.

"Does it have to be female?"

She chuckled, snorted slightly. "It does if you want silk."

"The males don't produce it?"

Keri vigorously shook her head so that her red locks fluttered. "No, the males are good for nothing except stealing insects from the female webs."

"What does the female do when the males try to steal?"

Keri hunched her shoulders. "Sometimes she attacks the male, but mostly she just ignores him."

"It mirrors my relationship with Dr. Keri." I looked behind me and saw the other tech was back, having replaced the spider wherever it would now sleep off its CO_2 hangover.

"Thank you," I said, and bowed.

The two techs returned my deference, and I looked to Doctor Anatole. He tried to smile, and the result was a wince. "Shall we adjourn to my office for a moment?" He asked.

"That sounds like a good idea." I turned to thank the twosome one last time, but they were already engaged with some paperwork and took no further notice of me. The tour was over.

The doctor and I left the room and walked down the hall. We stopped before a door painted in blistered coats of wintergreen. There was a tiny diamond-shaped window fitted at eye-level in the door, with a pane of pebbled glass seated inside the rhombus. He thumbed the entry port on the door. The light-emitting diode flashed from red to green and he led me inside.

The room was dominated by a walnut desk on which there was a letter opener and three porcelain monkeys who covered their eyes, ears, and mouths. It was a kitschy representation of the *See no evil, hear no evil, speak no evil* proverb. I didn't take the figurines as a fortuitous omen that this interview would go well, but the doctor wasted no more time.

"I understand you are now a private detective, Mr. Moglich." He walked around the desk and sat in a seat as straight-backed as an electric chair. "I assume Stelios Labs must at least be tangential to your investigation, else you wouldn't be here." He motioned toward a much smaller chair across from him. Its lesser dimensions were probably meant to give him the psychological edge with employees. This chair sat on a threadbare Persian rug that smelled of mothballs. I sat down in the smaller seat.

"At least three women have been killed by someone who I've been pursuing for a short time now, all of them within the space of a week."

The doctor winced. I didn't know if it was a tic or sympathy. "That's unfortunate."

"Whoever killed the women thought I was getting too close to him." I shifted in the seat. "He attempted to kill me with a bomb, the contents of which have been analyzed."

He leaned forward. He didn't seem suspicious or guarded, merely curious in his professional capacity as a man of science. I continued. "Precursor elements from the bomb led back here. These include certain threads of silk, the golden orb itself, as well as milk proteins." I clasped my hands together. This was my only lead left, and if he misinterpreted my gesture as a prayer offered to him he wouldn't have been that wide of the mark. "I'm not pointing fingers or questioning your own security measures, but I think someone who worked here or does work here is the culprit. Or they may be at least working with the culprit." I stood up from the chair, which creaked beneath me. "At the very least they know the killer."

Doctor Anatole nodded and stood with me. He stroked his chin. "Do you have any idea who this individual might be? A description?"

I thought about it and about Tmu Tarakan. "Eastern European or maybe Eurasian, probably male."

The doctor massaged his temples, as sometimes members of the older generation did when getting ready to use enhanced reality implants or prepping to check something in the general storage of their brains.

He paced, walking back and forth. I lost all my suspicion of him. He was merely an eccentric, the kind of person who gravitated to a nonprofit out of a sense of idealism. "Do you have anything else to go on?" He asked.

"How are the benefits here?" I asked "For your researchers and employees?"

His skin grew ruddy with anger, except for the necrotic flesh of the pock scars. "If you're implying that we don't pay our employees well enough, and that they therefore have to supplant their incomes with espionage-"

He wagged his finger and I countered the gesture with a wave of my hand. "That's not what I'm asking."

"What are you asking?" He huffed so heavily that a couple of grey hair from his nostrils peeked out and flailed.

"Do you have a dental plan?"

"Of course." His posture was ramrod.

"I need those records for comparison."

"It's against the law for me to disclose the personal information of our current employees."

"Let's start with former," I asked. "Do you have those cached?"

"Yes, but maybe the names aren't attached to the dental files."

"Well," I said, "we'll get an image and then I'll use my sketch artist mod to try and put a face to the teeth. If we get a face, then we'll try to put a name to it."

It was better to start the search for the killer among the former employees anyway, even if the records on them were only incomplete or partial. Those who'd been fired or who had quit were more likely to yield a culprit among their number. The "former employees" file would contain the disgruntled, vengeful, and the aggrieved.

He pressed his temples like an old fortune teller, and I stifled a laugh. At least he was subvoc literate, which was more than could be said for most people his age. He spoke out loud as he subvoc'd, and I figured it was too late for him to be corrected or to ever master the technology.

"Human Resources, Dental Index Access, Transfer to the implant of one Moglich, John."

I brought Denholm up from his sleep, or whatever his dreamless stasis was. "Denholm, I want you to compare the model you constructed from the bite marks retrieved from Kyra Boxer's breast to what Doctor Anatole just sent me. Check for a partial or full match."

"Yes sir."

I spoke to the doctor while Denholm worked. The older gentleman seemed fascinated by this process. I did my best to explain it to him. "He'll look for drill marks, fills, bridges, pulled teeth. If the perp worked here, we'll get at least a partial match."

Doctor Anatole shuddered, as if he'd just acquired the chills. He had sorrowful ancient features. "Dreadful to think that someone working here is a murderer." He shook his head, as if made an accomplice simply for hiring someone. Another thought crowded out questions of his own guilt. "What if he had his teeth replaced with dentures after working here, before biting the woman in question?"

I shook my head. "When you punch someone, that punch is coming from your core, not just your fist. It's the same with teeth. When you bite something, you're not just leaving an impression of your teeth, you're telling me about your jaw, your cheeks, everything."

"Incredible," the doctor said, his voice barely audible. Lazlo was right about those young punks. Here was a man of science bowled over by something pretty simple, whereas those youngsters who used their subvocs for sexting would merely yawn at what I was saying.

"There is a match, sir."

I wasn't sure if the doctor was listening to my subvoc, but he could read the reaction on my face. He smiled until the corners of his tired eyes creased. He rubbed the grey threads of hair over his liver-spotted head with the compulsive diligence of a housecat cleaning itself.

"Bring up ER for comparison," I said. A tomographic model of a mandible appeared, a rotating three-dimensional construct. It matched well with the file on the left side of my field of vision, which had come from the records the doctor had sent me after rubbing the salt-and-pepper sides of his head.

"Good, Denholm. Now warp the model to make sure the landmarks of the file from the doctor and the mold you cast from the bite both match up. Activate plastic surgery consult mod."

The doctor was confused by the volley between me and my butler. "I thought you said it was a sketch artist program?"

"It's used by police, but it was designed to build digital models for plastic surgery or for burn masks."

"Ah," the doctor said.

"Building the face that could potentially go on the teeth and jaws, sir."

Pixilated flesh formed in growing clusters of pinkish cells. There was no guarantee the suspect was Caucasian, but we had to start somewhere. I looked at the doctor and said, "The shape of the foot leads to a guestimate of the calf, which can get you a good approximation of how the thigh might look."

"But there it ends?" The doctor asked, a fearful edge to his voice. "You can't build a body from a footprint, can you?"

"Not yet."

His eyes were wide, nearly paralyzed from all the new information he'd been forced to take in. "A man would have to be a fool to commit a crime in this day and age."

"Either a fool or a genius," I said. "Although even geniuses make mistakes."

This one apparently did. "Color map complete, sir."

"Thank you, Denholm. Remain on standby for now."

"Certainly, sir."

I subvoc'd the image to the doctor's brain. "Check your enhanced reality mod," I said.

"Yes, detective."

Now I had to talk to him slowly, to treat him like a witness whose memory I needed to jog. The good news was that by priding himself on his job, he probably had as much incentive as I did to catch and punish our bite-happy bastard. What's more is that while victims sometimes needed cajoling out of their irrational fear of the perp's power, the good doctor hadn't been victimized; he'd only been played. Victims were scared. Fools wanted revenge.

"I recognize him," the doctor said.

"Name?" I asked, a lump in my throat the size of a black talon bullet.

"Matthew," the doctor said. "His name is Matthew Immer."

The word worked like a command and the file on the employee who was terminated for theft appeared, along with a photo eerily similar to the model we'd constructed based on shared info between the doctor and Denholm.

Matthew Immer was more boy than man. He was pale and runty, with hyper-alert eyes that were red around their orbits like those of a lab rat kept awake too long. My heart was beating rapidly now, punching like it was trying to erupt from my chest. This morning I had little to go on. Now I had a face and a name.

For the first time the fucker hadn't stonewalled me with some "digital watermark" spoof. He hadn't bothered to cover all his tracks because he figured he'd blow me up along the way while I was following his trail. But I was alive and still on his ass.

Denholm wasn't slumbering, so I didn't have to bother with saying his name to trigger the wakeup function. "Get me everything you can on Matthew Immer."

I turned back to the doctor, who was exhausted. He walked back to his throne and sat down. He sagged into an inert pile, as if he never again intended to stand. I went back over to the smaller chair and sat down in it across from him.

"Why did you fire him?" I asked. "I'm guessing it wasn't for stealing office supplies."

"Well, in a manner of speaking it was." Doctor Anatole wiped perspiration from his upper lip. "Although he wasn't stealing printer ink."

"What was he stealing?"

"Data on the transgenic silkworm project."

"If you had to hazard a reason, why would you say he would go for that? Stelios does other transgenic research."

"Oh yes. Of course," the man spluttered.

"What's so special about silkworms?"

He pointed toward the diamond pane nestled in his door, out in the direction of the corridor. "You heard Dr. Keri. Spiders don't play well with each other. Put eight golden orbs in a habitat together and in a month you'll have one banana spider fatted on seven others."

"Females eat females, too? I remember her saying they ate males."

"They eat everything." The doctor absently picked a booger from his nose. "Silkworms play nice with each other. They can be raised together." He pointed toward the far wall of his office. It was packed with bookcases filled with real paper antiques bound in Moroccan leather. "I never get complaints from the lab down there," the doctor said. "The silkworms don't even try to crawl away as long as they've got mulberry leaves. That's why they call them that, mulberry silkworms."

I didn't want to be rude, but I subvoc'd while he spoke. I brought up my ER viewer and requested GenEd to give me the lowdown on mulberry silkworms. A woman's voice spoke in my head. "Mulberry Silkworms are better known as *Bombyx mori*. They have been raised domestically for thousands of years in China. The popularity of sericulture dates back seven millennia."

"Pause," I subvoc'd. That would have to do for now. The doctor was as technologically naïve as they came, and he didn't notice that I had tuned out for a moment like a student during an interminable lecture.

"The profile on him said he had an IQ in the high genius range, and he came from the former Ukraine." Doctor Anatole snapped his fingers and pointed at me upon completion of the motion, a gesture meant to give me kudos for my initial guess on the culprit's nation of origin. "He behaved a bit rudely, a bit tone deaf socially even for someone in an environment as socially backwards as a nonprofit research facility."

"Was he sexually inappropriate with the females?" I asked.

Doctor Anatole loosened the half-Windsor on his paisley tie. "He was too awkward around the women to be inappropriate. In his reports, he was always in-depth and displayed a very keen wit. Subvocally he could probably thaw the defenses of the coldest heart, male or female."

"But face to face," my voice trailed off.

He picked up the thread. "Face to face, it was almost like," he struggled to describe the extent of Matthew Immer's social paralysis, as if he himself were crippled by proxy. "It was like he had Asperger's or mild autism." The doctor's gaze grew distant, and his voice faded with it. "But he was brilliant in the lab."

"I imagine." I'd already seen what he could do.

"He was an incel," Doctor Anatole said. "Involuntarily celibate." I didn't need the clarification, but I nodded anyway.

I stood from my creaking seat, coughing as a cloud of dust rose from the Persian rug beneath the chair's four legs. "I want to thank you for your time." I extended my hand across the surface of the walnut desk. We shook above the porcelain statue of the three monkeys.

We unclasped hands, and the doctor walked around his desk. I headed toward the door and he followed at my heels. "I think you may have saved a life," I said. The truth was he may have saved thousands or even hundreds of thousands of lives, depending on what Matthew Immer's next project was. I didn't want to tell that to the man, though. Schengen City had endured enough chaos for now, and if I added to his troubles it would only probably make the frail man tremble more.

He opened the office door for me, a serene grin plastered across his face. He'd done his good deed for the day.

As for me, I'd already bruised the killer's ego by living long enough to put this much of the puzzle together. It was time to destroy him. I would thereby keep my ass from rotting in Schengen Dungeon on a triple murder beef, or plummeting from Vasily Timofev's gyrocopter over the Casino Node and ending up impaled on the point of the Eifel Tower. That was at least how my death appeared to me in the last nightmare I'd had, which most certainly would not be the last.

CHAPTER FIFTEEN

IN THE SHADOW OF THE SNAKE

There was the crushing sound of rusted tin breaking in the vice of a steel maw. There was no train coming, so my companion and I got a good look at the city workers rampaging in their steel exoskeletons in the middle distance. The metal giants lumbered through a shantytown. They kicked over hovels and campfires, tearing through clotheslines strung with damp laundry as they marched.

I thought it was part of the general chaos that had held sway in the Nodes for the last few days- perhaps the mechs had gone haywire – but my comrade sitting with me in the maglev station set me straight. "It's business as usual."

The man's face was a weltered patchwork of skin grafts that hadn't taken. The color of the parts on his face that weren't burnt didn't match the tone of the exposed flesh of his limbs. The arms and legs looked to be cheap fedgov cybers. He was obviously a product of one of our many failed campaigns in the sandbox.

"They tear those coffin city camps up as fast as people can jerry rig 'em." He shook his head and showed remarkable dexterity as he licked the scarred remnants of his lips and rolled a cigarette with the PVC claws they'd given him in place of fingers.

I watched the carnage unfold beyond the Kevlar mesh fence strung on the far side of the maglev rail bed. "It looks like a new model of mech," I said.

One of the rampaging exoskeletons crushed a flaming oil drum in its pincers, sending embers heavenward. The light from the smoldering cinders stained the clouds in the sky a deep crimson. The vet nodded and lit his cigarette with a campaign flint lighter he kept in a hideaway compartment on his right hand. It was his body to do with what he wanted, but I thought the mod was tacky. "They call it the beachcomber. Someone awhile back sent a general frago blast to every open subvoc detailing all the weak points on the old raptor model. Fedgov had to adjust fire."

A bit of fiery debris floated into the sky, an old gasser car hood glowing like brimstone and carried on the wind. My comrade was unfazed. He had more faith in that Kevlar net than I did.

A voice from somewhere on the man's body betrayed his fear however. "Mild oxycodone release scheduled in twenty minutes."

"Shit." The man struggled with the hand not holding the cigarette to grope for the button on his person that would shut up the voice. The raptor exoskeleton wasn't apparently the only vulnerable machine in the Schengen.

The vet finally found what he was looking for in the region of his solar plexus. He pounded the button with a closed fist, not as if it was a toggle switch but was a bit of undigested food lodged in his throat. "Forgot to turn the external indicator off. Sometimes I sleep and the missus wants to ask me how I am without waking me up."

"I didn't hear it," I lied.

The eyes in the wound that was his face twinkled. "You want a hit of the smoke?"

I shook my head. He puffed and pointed the cherry of his fatty in the direction of the ghetto. The squatters below were invisible from the elevated snake platform, but the rocks they were throwing up at their foes were hard to miss. One even hit the thermoplastic guard bubble covering an operator inside his steel skeleton.

"They'll let 'em throw rocks." The vet nodded to himself and dragged his cigarette until his eyes squinted.

"What happens if someone fires a shot at them?" I asked.

He grinned. It was evident that even though violence had maimed him, he couldn't shake his taste for it. "Then they'll get the culprit's head in their grapplers and pop their noggin like a goddamn grape." The man flicked the butt of his smoke onto the rail-line. He turned to me. "Bet you wonder what an old fogey like me is doing risking his ass at a snake station at three a.m.?"

"You look like you can take care of yourself." I was hoping that would flatter him into silence, but it didn't. He flashed me a mouthful of porcelain choppers he'd probably gotten after losing the set he'd been born with in a pulse blast.

His hands went into the tiger-striped fatigues he wore, and out came two refurbished relics. I recognized both. I wondered if he knew that from where I was sitting it looked like he was pointing guns at me.

I decided to talk shop with him. That way he might think me a member of whatever brotherhood he considered himself a part of, instead of someone who was part of the conspiracy to screw him over. I pointed at the long-barreled arm on the left. "That's a Comanche forty-four."

"Good eye." He winked. From what I could tell the eye was an original, although there was a rosy tint to the left peeper that might not have been the reflection from the coffin ghetto under assault down below. If he was modded with a scope in his eye, he wouldn't need it to sight me and blast me at pointblank range.

"It's a hard gun to hide," I said. "I used to be a police officer, so I know."

The vet stuffed the gun back into its holster, which shined with a linseed gloss. "The thin blue line." He patted me on my left shoulder. He was probably too preoccupied with the piece in his right arm to realize the limb he touched wasn't any realer than his, although it was more expensive and had better function.

"What about this?"

He brandished the forty-five. Its nickel-plated cylinders caught sulfurous light from the transom above us.

I tried to adopt a wide cowboy drawl. "That there is the gun that won the West." My time in theme bars in the Casino Node had finally paid off.

"That's right." He pointed the gun down at the cement ground beneath us, which made me a little easier. "I don't know about the range on them mechs, but I'm not about to point a piece in their direction."

"I appreciate that." I didn't want to be turned into a puddle of gristle because of his shellshock. I thought about subvoc'ing a citizen's report to Cyber Therapy Centcom when I got the chance, since I figured it probably wasn't a good idea to have him walking the streets. If I was going to report every unstable member of the Schengen, then the population was going to be halved overnight.

"She's got to be cocked every time she's fired." He slowly drew back the hammer. "But I'm thinking of getting her modded so she can be fanned." He stroked his gendered gat. I wondered what her name was. I hazarded the moniker was double-barreled, maybe Lucy-Maye or Betty-Sue.

"I'm a responsible owner." He put the revolver into a stowaway compartment inside his fatigues. "I ain't leaving nothing to six pallbearers nor to twelve jurors."

I hated to ask questions since I was afraid that might cause him to display his heaters again, but now I was curious. "You got cams on those?"

"Damn skippy. Any time I shoot them, I got recordings for the authorities." He patted the guns beneath his jacket, stroking them through the camo as lovingly as a bitch cradling her pups. "I done peeled caps three times in three different Nodes, and all three were KIA notches."

The train was barreling toward us, and I shouted as the steel nose of the snake rushed forward. "How'd the cases come out?"

He snapped his fingers, and the hollowed core of his polymer hand echoed. "Three dismissals, jack. 'Justifiable homicide' are the two most beautiful words in the world."

The chrome doors opened and he stepped onto the car. I walked farther down the concrete padding of the station, and got on near the caboose. The doors closed, and Denholm's voice intruded onto my dark ruminations.

"Sir?"

"Talk to me."

There was a hiss and a start as the snake pulled out. "Sir, I have found some partials on Matthew Immer."

"Preach on it."

"This is from a KGB report, part of the bundle of documents declassified after the Federation failed."

Vasily Timofev might not have liked sectarianism since it cost his brother his head, but I had to thank the terrorists for chipping the empire into fragments since it was the only reason I was getting this report.

"Feed me," I said.

"Immer, Matthew was a Eurozone citizen who went to work for the Russians for ideological reasons redacted in the file." Denholm paused, skipping over the blackout portions of the document. "He worked in the Aralkum Desert."

My geography wasn't the worst, but that didn't ring a bell and I didn't want to bring up my GenEd mod while getting such critical info. "Where is that?" I asked.

"It is in what was once the Aral Islands, which eventually suffered total desertification."

"I wonder why our perp decided to make his career move there, then." I looked through the window, trying to discern more than the outline of a neon-poisoned tenderloin district where women who were more or less than human plied their trades. My breath fogged the window and I wiped the condensation away with my false fist.

Denholm brought me back to Earth, or thereabouts. "Sir, he was testing anthrax, tularemia, brucellosis, glanders, and various other dangerous viruses."

"Testing them on what?"

"Green monkeys, sir."

I took him literally at his word, but finally decided to bring up my GenEd mod. I laughed when I saw the real thing in my ER. I got an image of an old-world monkey, with golden fur radiant as the spots on the banana spider back in Stelios Labs. "The green monkey is actually gold," I subvoc'd to Denholm.

My GenEd mod informed me that green monkeys were sexually dimorphic, with the males being larger than the females. "Exactly the opposite of the golden orb spiders."

"What, sir?"

"Nothing, just talking to myself. Carry on, Denholm."

"According to a report given to someone with rank of Polkovnik-"

"Colonel," my lagging Babel translator and GenEd mod both corrected the word at the same time, and I felt schizophrenic.

"...he was working on an auto-fermenting nanobot." A small alloyed arachnid appeared in the file, although the steel spider was only four-legged. "The spider was programmed to convert seed stock of anthrax to billions of spores, via a fermentation process that wasn't successful and was scrapped by a General Jirov."

"Go on, or does the file end?"

"No sir," Denholm said. "The failure of the program was attributed to incompetency at a higher level. Immer was given high marks for ability and industriousness and he was then transferred to another division, where he was put in charge."

"What division?" I asked, rubbing the back of my neck. It had been a long day.

"Transgenic warfare."

That made me sit up. "What did he do there?"

"'God's work' and 'a miracle' according to the notes here."

"Specifically?" I wasn't interested in the praise of the bloodthirsty warmongers for their toy boys.

"He experimented with special additives to keep chemical agents from decaying when transported over great distances, in adverse conditions like zero G or negative two-hundred and seventy degrees Celsius."

I didn't know of anywhere on Earth that got that cold. Siberia was sunny Acapulco in comparison. "It sounds like they weren't content to poison the Earth, like maybe they wanted to wreck shop up in outer space too."

"Could be, sir," my friend allowed. "Shall I continue?"

"Please." I was curious to see exactly how busy our sociopath had been.

"Doctor Immer had moderate success with modified silkworm cocoons as a medium for 'bomblet conveyance and preservation.'"

"Doctor?" I said. "PhD?"

"No sir, or rather that in addition to an M.D. from Phillips of Marburg."

"So, educated in the heart of the Eurozone and turned pro in East Bumfuck or the Russian equivalent of the middle of nowhere. Tmu..." I struggled with recall the old fashioned-way.

"Tmu Tarakan, sir."

"Thank you," I said. The train stopped, but it was mere pro forma programming from higher. No one got on or off, at least not onto my car. "So our prodigy is moving up the rungs of the ladder. Why suddenly did he ghost? Did he flee when the Federation fell?"

"No sir."

"Espionage? Tired of getting all that state-endorsed egg and he wanted some of that private sector cream?"

"According to this file, there were problems that started manifesting after about a year in the transgenic sector."

"Let me guess. Not enough recreation, no ping-pong tables?"

"Sir, the suicide rate was astronomical. Vodkaism was also perceived as a problem." I guessed there was some sort of glitch in the Babel mod. Some idioms produced a one-to-one conversion. The English "To throw in the towel" would seamlessly convert to "Throw the shotgun into the corn," in most Euro dialects. Vodkaism was apparently untranslatable.

"Sir, there was even an incident of a report of a green monkey dying of acute alcohol poisoning."

"Sounds like somebody's conscience was eating away at them. You don't get a monkey drunk for no reason."

"It is abnormal behavior, sir."

"Anything on Immer's medical health?" I asked. "Anything psychological?" I'd already gotten a shortened diagnosis from Doctor Anatole back at Stelios earlier, but I was hoping to buttress that.

"He complained about the effect all the required vaccinations had on him." Denholm paused before enumerating. "He said his skin had lost all its lubrication. He was tested for allergies."

The train stopped again and the doors slid open on whisper quiet runners. It was another ghost platform, an empty station. "What kind of allergies did he have?"

"Would you like the full report?"

"Go ahead," I said.

"He lost all sense of smell and said he couldn't eat dairy or meat. He said his sinuses were constantly draining, and that his hair was permanently bleached by the peroxide used to sterilize various chambers via showerheads."

"What was the doctor's conclusion?"

"That it was all psychosomatic."

I highly doubted that all of it was psychosomatic. Either a man's hair was bleached or it wasn't. I knew mine was white from my time on the force and I had no desire to mod my badge of honor out of existence.

"What happened next?"

"He disappeared," Denholm said.

"No defection, no selling of secrets, reports of blackmail?"

"There were various unconfirmed sightings of him in locales as far-flung as the NAU and sovereign Quebec, but there was no hard evidence."

"A guy with his medical issues would have a hard time going incognito, unless he healed himself," I said. That was entirely possible. Someone with his skill and intelligence might be able to triage his wounds, although his soul and his conscience might still be dogging him.

The lights of the Casino Node drenched over the snake, luminous as a star going supernova. "Home sweet home." The doors opened and I stepped out. My wand chirped from inside my jacket, losing a tenth of a dark coin on the fare.

"Okay, Denholm." I was still in subvoc mode, and as I walked I scanned the light-bathed streets for signs of trouble. I ordered my ER to dim contrast and adjust tint, so that I wouldn't have to squint in the glare of the hustler's wheelhouse where I lay my head each night. The actual moon in the sky was no match for the luxury cruise dirigibles whose searchlights glowed with the megawatt power of a dozen false suns.

I walked toward the front of Zhakpot. I joined slot jockeys wearing rayon and rubber leisurewear as they pushed through the revolving glass doors gilded in dazzling gold trim. "I want you to do a six degrees ping on Immer, and then I want you to ping whatever names you find and give me any in the Schengen. If no names come up in a five hundred klick radius, I want you to extend the search until someone comes up."

There was very little chance of finding Matthew Immer directly, but I gave myself better odds if I could go through someone else to get to him.

A bellhop I knew by sight but not by name made his white-gloved hand into a gun and gave me a virtual shot to the gut. "Evening, Mr. Moglich."

"Evening," I said. I tried to smile at his gesture, although I'd had enough gunplay to last for quite a while and found it impossible to make my thumb into a hammer and my two fingers into a barrel. I had a sneaking suspicion the bellhop's name was Marky, but I didn't want to risk it. He wore his monkey suit well, whatever his name was. He quickly shined the golden buttons on his pelisse with a gloved hand, and then tipped his usher's cap slightly to give it the perfect rakish angle.

"Sir, one name comes up within a ten-mile radius."

I walked past the bank of copper elevators, and headed toward the service stairs. I pushed the door open and ascended the first flight of steps. The passageway was grim, but I wanted a bit of privacy. I also wanted to make my tail work, assuming I had one on my ass.

"His name is Cesar Montfort, sir. He is at Krauss Clinic."

"Why does that not surprise me?" Krauss was a dual cybertherapy/research facility, designed to use existing treatments to cure cyberpsychosis and to develop new treatments based on whatever they learned in the praxis phase. I was familiar with it from the time I got "bleed" (as the doctor called it) from my ER mod. I lost control over when and how to summon my display and how to make it hibernate again. I walked around for two days in a delirium, random GenEd and GedMed files appearing before my vision like hallucinations. Images of rare forms of cancer competed with holograms of extinct marsupials, and I couldn't see well enough to take a piss in a pot.

I sweated as I climbed the stairs, and paused on the landing to adjust my left arm. The limb had become partially unsnapped from its harness and was chafing the neoprene liner over the fleshy stump at my shoulder joint.

"What's this Montfort's relationship to our quarry?"

"Sir, he worked with Matthew Immer during the early stages of his career with the Kremlin. His job, according to the same declassified files, was to procure healthy specimens for testing."

"Green monkeys?"

"Yes sir, but because he was in procurement he traveled constantly. That caused concern for the aforementioned general, since defection was always a top operation security concern. He underlined 'always,' sir."

"I guess he meant 'always,' in that case." I heard that satisfying snap that meant the arm was popped back into the joint. "Their fears were well-founded then?" I started walking again. "It sounds like Cesar defected." I hadn't met him, but we were already on a first name basis.

"He had a psychotic breakdown," Denholm said. "He was placed in a state facility, escaped, and made his way here."

"How did Krauss get him?" I figured maybe he volunteered to be a guinea pig. He was probably lucky that the regime he'd fled was collapsing around the time he was losing his mind. If the Kremlin hadn't had larger problems on their hands and they were afraid he might spill state secrets, he would either be extradited by mutual treaty or extracted by force and then killed. People who worked on programs designed to kill millions didn't have qualms about snuffing out one psycho.

I started climbing the staircase again. I assured my burning limbs that I was almost home. Room service and a hot bath were in order. "Sir, a judicial ping reveals he was involuntarily committed after slicing his wrists open with a broken bottle in Greenspace Park."

"Poor bastard." I stopped in front of the landing before my door, and slicked my white hair back with perspiration I gathered from my forehead in my tired hands. I opened the door with my sweaty palm and walked to my hotel room.

"He was arrested once before that for making terroristic threats against Stelios."

"Stelios?" There was a connection I hadn't expected to crop up, at least until I thought about the animal rights angle.

"Yes sir, they have some gibbons on hand. They insist they're only there for transgenic purposes, but the Green Guerillas believe they're conducting tests and they've targeted them for bombings."

"Did the Greens carry out any attacks?"

I let my clammy thumb drift over the door to my digs. Red became green.

"No sir, although a Guerilla's name does come up in a news item that also mentions Montfort."

"Let's hear it." I opened the door. "Honey, I'm home."

Maybe it was a matter of pride, but Denholm never responded to that. "Ultimate Che was arrested for attempting to cut down a bioluminescent tree in protest of GMOs and what he claimed was their especially toxic effects on the homeless seeking shelter in Loomoo Park."

"Ultimate Che." That drew the first belly laugh from me in a while. "I'm guessing that's not what it says on his birth certificate."

"I can access his birth certificate," Denholm offered.

"That's not necessary." I walked over to the bed and flopped into the already molded contours, a pharaoh laid to rest in his memory foam sarcophagus. "What did Ultimate Che have to say about Cesar Montfort?" I gave myself bonus points for not laughing as I said the name this time.

"He was interrogated in the Schengen Dungeon and claimed that Cesar Montfort had approached him, while the latter was busking in Greenspace."

"That was the same place where he eventually tried to off himself with shards from a glass bottle."

"Yes sir," Denholm said.

"What did Cesar want Che to do?" It sounded like the premise to a joke with a lame punchline.

"He wanted him to deliver a message to Doctor Gennady Anatole."

"Hey, I met him today."

"Yes sir."

I unzipped my clamshell jacket and threw it toward the ground. The shag of the carpet was so deep and the fabric so soft that I could step out of the shower, air-dry in the nude, and be warm as an iguana on a sunstone in under a minute. "What message did Cesar want our dilettante terrorist to deliver to the good doctor?"

The pause let me know Denholm was going to be quoting verbatim. "'Hurt any more monkeys and I'll kill all of you.'"

I thought of the golden-furred monkeys again and wondered how they got saddled with their name. "Call Kraus and try to set up an appointment for tomorrow morning." I adjusted the gel levels on my pillow to take it from cool to arctic to help with the pain in my neck. Then I closed my eyes and drifted off to sleep. My first dream was of a capuchin helper monkey wearing a bellhop suit and screaming from his perch on the shoulder of an organ grinder I was sure was Cesar Montfort.

CHAPTER SIXTEEN

MY CYBERPSYCHOSIS QUARRY

San Lazaro was the first church I had seen that incorporated bioluminescence in stained glass windows. There were bars over the windows since we were in a rough part of town, but it was still possible to admire the way the sores on the saint's legs glowed like rubies and how his halo looked to be composed of triangular wedges of light ripped directly from the sun.

The front door to the church, made of stained oak, creaked open. Refugees in gray and brown wool staggered out to make their way toward the soup kitchen across the street. The sisters who had probably knitted their secondhand clothes followed quickly behind them in the dark. A strong wind picked up force and almost pulled one the penguin's veils off her head.

I walked down the street toward Krauss Clinic. I stopped before the entrance and let the movement sensor flicker to life and scan me. The clinic was built like a bomb shelter, composed of reinforced masonry that was ash-colored in the night.

"Identity confirmed," a voice said.

The doors to the bastille opened, and I walked inside.

"Good evening, Detective." The warden of this particular madhouse walked toward me. He was beetle-browed enough to look like an alien hominid pulling off the act of being human. "I'm Mr. Gentry." His smile was affable and his skin was oddly tanned for someone who worked nights and indoors.

"Thank you for seeing me." I followed him down a brick corridor that smelled of must. There were fissures in the brick that made me think about collapse and feel claustrophobic. The bright lights above us gave the hallway the look of an approach to a death house.

"My assistant informs me that you don't usually allow patients to have visitors not already on their approved list."

He half-turned to me while still making his way forward, exposing a gap between the nape of his neck and his dress shirt. "We never allow unapproved visitors for patients, even in a crisis."

I was confused. We stopped before the door, and he opened it saying, "Montfort was a fifty-one fifty, involuntary hold." Mr. Gentry preceded me into a less cloistered space. The floor was tiled cement with a manhole-sized grate in the center of the room. I looked up and saw showerheads spot-welded to the ceiling.

"That is a holdover from another time," Mr. Gentry said. He clearly didn't want me to get a gothic Bellevue vibe from the place and think this was where patients were hosed down. He pointed to the other side of the room, where a two-way mirror the size of a bay window was fitted into a wall.

I walked forward. "How long has he been a patient?" I still didn't see Cesar Montfort. I moved toward his enclosure cautiously, as if he were an exotic animal sleeping in a zoo exhibit that might appear from nowhere in front of me before the glass.

"He was a patient with us for three years." Mr. Gentry walked until he stood next to me in front of the two-way viewing window. A sound came from down the hall, and a night watchman in a leather bomber jacket pushed a computer console on a wheeled tray toward us.

The security guard nodded to Mr. Gentry, whose return nod sent the watchman away. "Two of those years were involuntary," the warden said. "The third year he was on a self-commit basis."

"So he's not a patient now?"

My host shook his head, slightly put out with me. "I told you that you wouldn't even be allowed here to see him if that was the case."

"What is he, then?" Just as I spoke of him he appeared, walking from a dark tunnel nestled in the far cinderblock wall of his chamber. He walked through his room, which had the dimensions of a double-coffin modular home with basic Murphy amenities.

"He's a subject," Mr. Gentry said. He stepped around me, to the computer his underling had wheeled in.

I looked at Cesar. He continued to ignore us, even though I had the sneaking suspicion he knew he was in a fishbowl. At least I hoped he knew he was still a test subject. If he was crazy enough to think he was somewhere else, then I might not get any actionable info out of him.

Cesar Montfort suddenly looked up. He didn't look toward me, but in the direction of the ceiling and the area around his head. It was as if he was using echolocation to find a fly. His hair was a radiating shrubbery of unwashed spirochetes. The dreadlocks were the size of sausages and framed the widest set of eyes I'd ever seen. He didn't look capable of blinking.

"He will not talk directly to you," Mr. Gentry said, tapping away on his keyboard. "He fears face to face interactions. He'll only communicate through an avatar." The warden turned the computer monitor toward me, on which there was a mirror image display of the room where Cesar Montfort sat. The only difference was the Cesar in the virtual room had been replaced with his polar opposite. On screen was a massive hulk of a barbarian instead of the lanky test subject. The warrior was something dredged from a teenaged boy's fantasy realm where he slayed dragons and rescued damsels.

"I knew you were coming," Mr. Gentry grinned, "so I decided to give him an avatar that would help him build confidence." He pointed to the knight on the screen. "That's this chap here."

I looked at the monitor. "I'll bet he's a hit with the ladies."

The warden's smile faded. "No, we haven't gotten him to the point where he's willing to interact with women. He's rarely even cooperative with men."

"What's his level of cooperation contingent upon?"

The warden's eyes flashed as if he was happy I'd prompted him with the right question. I crowded closer to the computer and he said, "It depends on which avatar you pick."

Gentry brought up a sidebar and started scrolling through an endless gallery of men, women, and children, even pets and inanimate objects. I looked back over toward Cesar in his cell. He was still staring at his computer screen.

"He wasn't always like this," I said, half-rhetorically. He couldn't have been like this and managed to busk in Greenspace Park.

"It would take up too much of my time for me to explain to you exactly what kinds of tests we're conducting here. In brief, Mr. Montfort has given his consent to allow us to tamper with the myelin sheath of his brain as well as the white matter."

"To what end?"

"To monitor addiction, for one."

I nodded. I had spent the last few years living modestly in a casino. If I hadn't learned something about addiction and how to avoid it, I would be sleeping in a coffin in one of the numerous squatter camps.

"Mr. Montfort and our research team are interested in the mind's addiction not to normal drugs or chemicals, but to information itself. It is not the rarest form of cyberpsychosis."

"What is the psychosis he's suffering from?" I asked.

"Opting out," Gentry pointed through the glass, at Cesar still playing on his computer. "If one spends enough time with virtual blandishments they forget what reality is. Mr. Montfort spent half a year looking through every non-encrypted image yielded by his subvoc pinging for 'attractive woman.'"

My eyes widened. Gentry nodded to confirm it. "About two-hundred and sixty-three thousand minutes locked inside his own brain, essentially lifeless except for the ability to feel us feeding nutrients into his body or disposing of his waste while he was immobile."

"And when he came out of this state?"

"He couldn't look a woman in the eye."

"I see," I said. I nodded toward the computer. "Do you mind?"

"Be my guest." Mr. Gentry stepped aside. I used the mouse to scroll through the avatars. I decided to avoid the women, and I was thinking maybe even humans might be a bad bet. I scrolled past a mustachioed construction worker and a businessman in a grey suit with a striped tie.

"What are you doing with him right now?" I asked.

"We've tweaked him with a galvanizer."

"To do what?"

"He has a hypochondriasis mod installed, a deliberate somatoform virus. He must research thirty illnesses per hour. When he cannot find thirty in sixty minutes, he will be galvanized hard enough for muscular contraction until he screams." Mr. Gentry grinned, tasting the flavor of his own sadism as he smiled.

"And then what?"

His smile widened. "And then he is given a test to assess his recall. If he can prove his level of retention as adequate or better, he gets an hour break."

I was afraid to ask what would happen if he failed his test. Mr. Gentry was happy to confirm my fears without me needing to ask. "If he fails, there is a one in sixty chance we deliver a shock strong enough to induce defibrillation."

"But you could kill him."

"He's hemlocked," Mr. Gentry said, applying the brakes on my protest. "These experiments wouldn't be legal if he didn't have the euthanasia mod."

I was well-traveled. I was a student of cruelty, maiming, and death. Nevertheless, I thought shooting someone was far more humane than this kind of torture. I forgot for a moment that I was an investigator and that it was best to have this man on my side, since he could throw me out if the whim struck him and then I would be screwed.

"Whose idea was this? Yours?"

Gentry pointed through the glass. "His."

"Why?"

He smiled so that I could see the spit shining on the fanged points of his eyeteeth. "He'll only say he deserves to suffer. That 'I deserve to be a test subject for what I've done.' He won't elaborate."

Cesar didn't have to elaborate, not for me to get what I wanted from him. I put the cursor in the "Search" field on the sidebar at the right. "How many creatures do you have in here?"

Mr. Gentry chuckled. His interest was evidently piqued by my use of the word "creatures." He stood over my shoulder. "Not going with a human, huh?"

I looked at him, keeping my lips sealed until he answered me. "Any species with a proven taxonomy is in there." He rolled his eyes. "Be a botfly if that be your druthers."

"I just might," I said, typing "Green monkey." The little-golden furred, gibbon-sized monkey with the red eyes appeared. I looked back at Gentry. "How do I get that monkey in the room with him?" I pointed at the warrior on the screen, but naturally meant Cesar.

"Double-click. Although be advised," Gentry warned, "he is fickle and may not give you anything. In some ways due to the tampering with the myelin sheath of his brain, he is suffering from a kind of artificially-induced delayed maturation. His mirror neurons are not functioning well right now, and the orbital frontal cortex area of his amygdala is touch-and-go."

"Which means?"

"Which means you're dealing with a teenager at best, and a not so compliant or empathetic one."

I wasn't so worried about that. The most the barbarian could do was slay my little monkey. That would have negligible effect in the real world but would probably give Cesar a confidence boost, though probably not enough to approach a woman even in He-Man mode.

"Okay," I said, double-clicking my monkey into the room.

The barbarian stepped back, as if afraid. I heard a shriek from the room behind the glass of the two-way mirror, but I didn't look up. I glanced at Gentry. My hands were sweating as if they held a gun, not a mouse. "Should I type?"

"You can subvoc. His is always running."

"Please," a strident voice whined. He even sounded like a teenager. "I'm sorry," Cesar said to the monkey.

"You can make this better. You can repent," I said, "for what you and Matthew did in the Aral desert, at Tmu Tarakan."

The barbarian's back was already pressed against the far wall of his double-coffin accommodations. "How do you know about him? How do you know about that place?"

"You killed me," I said, "but you can make it right."

I heard weeping from the room, though the warrior avatar remained stoic. "I didn't want you to suffer anymore."

"I know," the golden monkey said. "And I don't want you to suffer anymore, either."

"What can I do?"

"Did Matthew ever tell you about his plans to flee?"

"Yes, we were close. We were so close that I think I sort of became Matthew, or at least I took on some of his traits."

"How so?" His fear seemed to be lessening. The warrior walked slowly toward the monkey, and stooped down. I allowed him to pick me up and cradle me in his arms. He rocked his golden-furred pet from side to side, as if it was somehow therapeutic for him to do so.

He spoke to the monkey snuggled tight to his chest. "Matt was scared of women. He was an incel."

I tried to remember where I had heard that word before. I'd heard it once from Doctor Anatole at Stelios Labs, but I'd also heard it somewhere else. "Involuntarily celibate," I said, as if sounding out the words that constituted the acronym could jog my flagging memory.

"He was so scared of women that higher said no females could be in the lab when he was. His hands would start shaking, he would drop phials and beakers."

I doubted that bothered the apparatchiks. A man with no lust for women was less likely to sell secrets for old school "honeypot" tricks. Also he would be distraction-free.

"Was he gay?"

"No," Cesar said, "just scared of women and he couldn't get over it. He said he'd been that way since he hit puberty."

"When he talked to you about fleeing, did he mention any plans? A mod or some surgeries?"

"He had a fear of going under the knife. He said he hated anesthetic."

"And no mods?"

"Matthew was a bricks and mortar guy," Cesar said. "He prided himself on being able to read, do long division in his head, write cursive, the works. He went to Marburg Uni."

"That's impressive. So, did he ever express admiration for anyone else who learned the old-fashioned way?"

"Yeah, he talked about Bernard Blankstone a lot. He even got a model kit for one of the mansions Blankstone designed, from the Starchitect Series."

"There wasn't a lot to do in your downtime at Aralkum?"

"Masturbation, suicide, vodka…" He trailed off. I was sure he could enumerate more forms of recreation. "How do you know about Aralkum? You're just a monkey."

"I'm the ghost of a monkey you killed Cesar, but I want you to know that I'm happier where I am now. I just came to tell you that I don't want you to carry anymore guilt for what you-"

Mr. Gentry shoved me away from the computer, seething. "What the hell are you doing? You're a detective. So, fine, ask questions. Leave therapy to the staff."

I straightened myself up to my full height. I wondered if I cracked him in the jaw if I would be able to handle the orderlies, that night watchman, and whatever else Kraus Clinic could throw at me before spoofing my way out of this dungeon with a little help from Denholm.

"Okay," I said. "I apologize." I breathed slowly, let my heartrate slacken. I knew that Cesar was sick, and Gentry was evil. A sick man in the hands of an evil man was too often the case in medicine, but it was something I shouldn't have let stand unchecked in this instance. I'd been here for only the better part of an hour, but that was more than enough time to sum up what was going on here hidden from view. Gentry was cultivating Montfort's guilt, feeding it to get him to sign off on being a willing guinea pig in their torture chamber. They probably weren't even paying him either. If any useful application came from this Schengen version of the Spanish Inquisition, I bet Cesar Montfort wouldn't see credit or dark coin one.

I hoped that maybe I had planted the seed for him to forgive himself and that he believed that pixilated apparition of a monkey was in fact a ghost come to absolve him of his crimes and to ease his conscience.

It certainly didn't sound like it though. "Mama!" He let out a piercing shriek. It was something like what one would expect from an infant starving for milk if the baby had been blessed with the vocal chords of a man racked by the pain of life.

"Mama!" Cesar shouted again, and I turned away. I couldn't open that door fast enough, or bolt down the corridor with enough speed to escape the pleading screams for a mother who wasn't coming.

"Wonderful," Mr. Gentry's voice echoed down the hall. "Now he's fully regressed." I stowed the urge to turn around and use my cybered fist to morph Gentry's face into a red paste of pâté and shattered bone shards. I opened the door to the outer courtyard. My mind was twisted and contorted by this investigation so far, but I had finally seen a light out of the maze. I walked forward and remembered where I'd first heard about incels, before coming to this madhouse or going to the spider silk research lab.

It was time to head back to the Green Node.

CHAPTER SEVENTEEN

INCOMMUNICADO

The route I took to the Civic Plaza was different this time. I got off two stops earlier in the Green Node to shake any tails that might be on me, or at least to confuse them. I walked in silence, moving through greenfield soggy as bog. My hushpuppies were soaked to the point where they would probably need to be resoled when I got home, if I got home.

It was quiet, and dark under the thick canopy of old growth trees gathered around me. I didn't see any cyclists or walkers, which made me think I had maybe wandered into a wildlife corridor of some kind. The grasshoppers chirped and an owl hooted to protest the invasion of a human on its turf.

I wasn't packing my gun, knowing that I wouldn't be able to get into the civic center with a heater on me. I figured that I would be conspicuous enough without carrying a piece. I did have my crystal icepick dagger. It would beat any metal detecting wand and could poke through bone like it was nuked cheese.

I wasn't sure what an incel was supposed to look like, but I was sure I carried the haggard air of someone with an ex-wife or two. Celibacy would probably have been an improvement.

A whispering noise rippled from the ground at my feet. I looked down in the blue light of the moon, expecting to see that I'd gone from soggy ground to a creek bed. Instead I saw the mouth of a runoff leading to a rushing stream. The water flowed toward the storm water drain of what looked like a power plant. Squinting without the aid of Denholm's eyes allowed me to barely make it out as a hydroelectric station in the distance.

Some of the kids were said to use these rapid flows and inlets to surf when the water level was high, and hydroplane on skateboards when the tide was receding. The occasional story of a drowning, an electrocution, or even a maiming in rotors or gears sometimes cropped up in my scream feed. It struck me as needlessly stupid behavior, but people rode the tops of maglev cars and threw rocks at beachcombers too.

"Shit," I whispered. If my shoes took on any more water, I was going to take them off, turn them over and drain them.

I broke through the tree line, cringing as I felt the cold seepage work its way between my toes.

The back of the civic center building was before me. I'd assumed that only the dress of the partygoers would be different this time, but an entire inflatable moonwalk skin had been stretched over the brick shell of the building as well. This gave the center the impression of an off-world military base. I guessed these men being shy also meant they needed extra protection, and maybe the rubber castle provided that cover for them.

I merged into the crowd of young men. They didn't look unusual, and I wouldn't have been able to form much of an opinion of them without having my a priori knowledge of their problems. I guessed the mean age to be about twenty or twenty-one. That would make Matthew Immer a little bit old for this crowd, assuming he was here. It would also make him easier to find though, if he was in fact mingling with the throng.

My heart was racing, my anger at the murders I'd witnessed in the back of my mind. I wanted to plant the point of my crystal toothpick in the killer's brain stem and watch the life leave his eyes.

There was only a low murmur among the boys, like monks at matins. They moved in groups of blanketed bunches. They wore plaid pajamas and silk onesies. There was even a little cosplay fun to the proceedings, with one young man toking on a Meerschaum that blew bubbles. I looked down and saw plush slippers to go with the PJs, snowy bichon heads and shaggy bear claw fur boots.

The door was manned by a bouncer who stood two heads taller than me and at eye level with the frame of the door he guarded. He was a lantern-jawed young man who wore a marine fleece sleeping outfit. A few other boys making their way toward the door wore similar Snuggly suits, and I wondered if there weren't some furries among them and if that might not be the problem. Maybe they could find the courage to approach women, but only if everyone involved in the courtship ritual was dressed like stuffed animals.

I queued up in line with the boys, and pulled my sticker from my jacket. "What's the cover tonight?" I spoke to the back of the head of the boy in front of me.

His friend turned back to me. He bore the look of someone who'd been hit too hard by puberty all at once, with bullet-sized pimples on his face and an Adam's apple as big as a golf ball. "He's incom," the boy said of his friend.

"Incom?" We shuffled forward.

"He can't talk unless he's known you for a year or so."

"Oh."

"The fee's two dark or a quarter credit."

"Thank you," I said, and shifted my selector switch to the right. I had the excess credits to trade.

The helpful young man patted his silent friend on the shoulder, and fell back toward me. He placed the arms of his velour snuggle suit together, which concealed his hands in the manner of a fur muffler. "If you try to do an interview, they'll throw you out," he said.

"No, I'm not here to interview anyone." I tried to think fast on my feet. "One night in the tenderloin I had my arm ripped off by a female Real Love worker whose program went haywire." I pulled up my left sleeve, and tapped the arm. "I haven't been able to talk to a woman since." I let my sleeve slide back down, and we shuffled forward together. We were almost to the door. Soft blush neon poured from the entrance, warm and pink.

"I thought you were a solo for one of the scream outfits." He pointed at my semiformal work clothes. "They love to do stories on us, but we just want to be left alone." He pointed at the doorman. "They get bounced quickly if they try that shit."

The boy waved wand to wand with the doorman, and passed through. The bouncer glared at me, but he didn't say anything. I resisted the urge to say "I'm not here to do an interview," since that was just the kind of ploy a muckraker might pull. I paid and walked in. I thanked God that I didn't get patted down and I got to keep my crystal poker.

All the S & M exhibits from the last event were gone. They were replaced by Real Love models like the ones I'd just mentioned, although these girls were programmed for nonsexual acts. Some of them were modded with tails and elven ears, and wide spheroid anime eyes. The women flitted between the groups of boy-men, talking to them and in some cases touching them on their shoulders or cheeks.

The voice of my new friend reached my ear. "This is where incels can practice their social skills with women." He walked down the same stairs I'd treaded with Russel Nadler. This time the ground was covered in a rubberized sheet that was coated red like a giant tongue unfurling from a mouth, or a slide in an amusement park.

"What's your name?" I asked.

"Jeremy."

The buoyant floor lifted us along as we walked, giving me a spring in my step whether or not I wanted it. "Are there any real girls here?" I changed posture, cringing a bit and hunching my shoulders to give my cover story a bit of cred. "I have to say, I'm a bit scared of the Real Lovers for the reason I talked about." I clutched my left arm in my right hand.

"I don't blame you," Jeremy said. We reached the ground floor of the convention hall. "Especially with the way everything's been going nuts in the Nodes."

I scanned the ranks of the young men in pajamas who were mingling with the women made of silicon and latex. Some of the women were dressed like exotic dancers, in feather boas laid over rhinestone-studded hot pants and fishnet stockings. Others wore blouses, pantsuits, and jumpers. They all passed muster with me, certainly looking more realistic than the Lovers I'd seen when I'd been young enough to wander into the Red Light and sleep with one.

I was uncomfortable as I walked through the uncanny valley, and I couldn't understand how this could be less disturbing than dealing with real women. It was one thing to fuck something that wasn't real. To talk to something that wasn't real didn't sound healthy. Then again, I was a detective and not a shrink.

I heard one faux female say, "Yeah, I'm studying bioengineering at Schengen Tech. Do you go to school?"

The boy to whom she'd put the question trembled in place. He opened his mouth to speak, and a pool of urine formed in the front of his pajama pants. The young man collapsed to the floor and the female bot stepped back, something in her programming telling her to disengage now that she'd incapacitated him with her simple query.

"It looks like a rough life," I said.

Jeremy didn't seem fazed that one of his comrades had already fallen out while the night was still young. I wondered what would happen if a real woman entered their midst. I was curious to see if they would be able to tell the difference between her and the Real Love models, even if she remained silent as she walked among them. Could she say "Hello" to them or even pass by them with the odor of a real woman on her, without them dropping like flies? Maybe that was part of this holistic treatment. I figured that perhaps the event organizers told the boys the girls were all machines, and then they snuck in a few real females to acclimate them.

"You asked about real women?" Jeremy brought me out of my thoughts.

"Yes," I said.

"There." He pointed toward the far side of the convention floor. There was a line of nervous boys in sleepwear waiting to step into something with the dimensions of a confessional booth, although it was made of partially enclosed cubical panels. One young man left the cube with two Real Love women dressed like flight attendants carrying his limp body away. The features of his youthful face were twisted in agony, but it was pain tempered by pleasure as if he'd just had an ecstatic revelation. Maybe he had. My wife had made me forget women were magic. These boys couldn't forget, because their terror wouldn't let them.

I realized that the cubicle was set up roughly where the synesthesia chamber had been when Viva Jasmine tested her mettle. I thought of her, and came back to the moment. "How do these guys get through their days?" I asked. I didn't see how they could go to the grocery store or ask directions in a world in which more than half the population was female.

"How does anyone get through the day?" Jeremy asked. "Mods, they mod their way through."

"Filters?" I asked. I knew about political ones, but that was the extent of my knowledge. I'd been in law enforcement my whole life, so facing the ugly was something I needed to do to earn my living. Filters had never been an option for me.

"They have mods that make everyone appear as male."

"They keep their ERs on twenty-four seven?" I asked. That might have been part of what was making them so crazy.

Jeremy nodded, and then tilted his head as he added, "Except when they're here, then they shut their defenses down or at least lower them."

And end up carried out by two attendants, I thought. "So mods can be used here though, right? There's not a break beacon?"

"No," Jeremy said, "there's no block." He pointed up toward the catwalk above us. "There's an override switch that Mr. Nadler will throw if someone tries an ident catcher or an unauthorized credit swipe is detected in progress, but other than that it's up to us whether to go naked or modded."

I gazed around the room saturated in dreamy light like a coral bed. The boys didn't look unhappy to me, at least as long as they confined themselves to talking to each other. Then again this was a special time, and it may have been for only one hour per week that they got relief from their torture. At every other moment they coped by programming reality until it became a livable lie.

All my GenMed mod told me was that there was a high rate of self-mutilation among the incels and that their rate of hemlock modding was twice that of the general population. They were also four times as likely to join Die Off and petition for involuntary mass extinction. Many of them went so far as to get vasectomies with parental consent. These operations were not of the mod variety that could be undone, but rather were old-fashioned knife jobs. I doubted Matthew Immer had done that to himself if he had as much fear of the knife as Cesar Montfort claimed.

I turned to Jeremy, who I thought seemed like a genuinely nice young man. "I need some time alone," I said. It sickened me when I had to spoof a human, but I made as if to pretend a panic attack was imminent just so that I could get some space.

"Sure," he said, and patted me lightly on the shoulder. "I've got to go find Danny anyway."

"Danny?"

"Yeah, he's the incom I came in here with." He grinned so that dimples formed on his face. "I can't even get him to talk to one of the Lovers, but one day I'm going to get him to go in there." He pointed toward the cubicle, out of which another unconscious boy was now being carried by two synth women.

"Good luck," I said.

"Thanks."

He disappeared among the boys, and I subvoc'd to Denholm. "Bring up the facial model we built at Stelios, plus Immer's employee badge photo and any Kremlin file photos you have."

"Yes sir."

"I want you to scan every face in here and tell me if you get a partial match or a full lock from any of these guys."

"You can count on me, sir."

It was possible that even if Immer was here that he had his own subvoc tap going and that he could hear me, or that he had even lured me here in the hopes of springing some kind of trap. I'd done what I could to shake a tail on my way in here, but no plan was foolproof.

"Sir–"

I got hit from behind so hard that my link with Denholm flat-lined and I fell to the ground. Feet stomped around me and one of the boys emitted a high pitched girlish shriek. I reached in the clamshell and gripped my diamond knife, expecting my attacker to be standing over me. That bum rush had hit me with the force of a linebacker, and I knew none of the kids could have done it.

"Look out, he's got a gun!"

The wind was still gone from my lungs, and I couldn't protest that it was only a knife I held. The Node was probably still on alert since Vasily's goon had sucker-punched a cyclist after landing in his gyrocopter, and now I was going to be made into an example.

No one moved though, at least not around me. I slowly got to my feet, and saw a large man bowling the young incels over as if they were marionettes being severed from their strings as he passed them. While they couldn't look a woman in the eye without hyperventilating, I hazarded the heavy wading through their midst could rape a woman without losing a night's sleep.

I heard a pneumatic whine, and I knew what it meant. I hit the deck again, and then the mechanical whirring gave way to Dread X rounds unloading from a handheld minigun. Jets of blood flew from an unfortunate incel whose head shattered in the next moment so forcefully that the red spray hit us all like a lawn sprinkler. The Real Lovers exposed themselves as machines now, walking in place and turning around in confusion since they had obviously not been programmed for combat.

The minigun kept firing and split one of the working girls in half, exposing her iron skeleton beneath the silicon. The upper half of her body flew across the room after being caught with several shells. Her torso was only a couple of feet from me. She looked at me and winked. "I think you're pretty cute, and I bet a lot of other girls would think you're cute too."

The gunner ran in my direction and then leaped over me. His Aracon metal mesh jacket was tanned to look like leather, and it fanned out around him as he jumped and picked up drag. I stood and ran after him as he reloaded another drum he kept inside his jacket. I was still looking at the back of his neck as I ran and pulled the diamond-skinned stabber from inside my clamshell. I didn't have to see the face to know he was one of the lackeys in Vasily Timofev's army. It was the same one from our little whirlybird ride awhile back.

I rushed after him, the dagger in my hand. I had no intentions of trying to stab him, since I was fairly sure that my knife would break on his hide like an acupuncture needle trying to pierce titanium. He was modded six ways to Sunday, and he had a gun that could turn me to mulch in three-tenths of a second with one slight pull of his finger on the hair trigger.

The truth was that I was only running after him because he was chasing someone else. My subvoc had recovered after taking that collision, and Denholm's voice was in my ear. "Sir, the combination of file photo, corporation nametag photo, and constructed image have identified the fleeing man as Matthew Immer to within 99.999 percent certainty."

I was running too hard to thank Denholm.

CHAPTER EIGHTEEN

VEERING TOWARD THE EDGE

People in the Green Node had good health insurance, so when they got shot the paras came. Vasily's thug was chasing Matthew Immer, who was hiding on the other side of a Medivac Air Fox that had just touched down. The thug crouched behind a second Air Fox and put his minigun back in his leather jacket. He reached into another pouch on his coat, bringing out something with the dimensions of a Needlegun.

"Help!" Incels screamed and maybe things were dire enough for even some of the incoms to be crying out, finally cured by this chaos. I ran until I was behind the heavy white Daimler Benz shell of the med vehicle.

Vasily's thug stood and squeezed a round in the killer's general direction. He ducked back down a second later, and shouted to be heard over the sound of the four vector thrust turbofans on the Air Fox as they cooled. "Thanks for leading us to this guy." He nodded in the direction of Matthew Immer hidden behind the other aircraft.

"Yeah but if you blow his brains out, Vasily can't use him." Unless it was just a mod they wanted, in which case they could blow his head open and scoop it out. But those heavy miniguns rounds were likely to burst metal as well as bone.

He tapped the minigun hidden in his Aracon jacket. "That was for the crowd." He waved the smaller gun in his right hand. "This is for him. And…" He studied what looked like a wristwatch on his arm. "I got him."

"A tracker?" I asked.

"Old-fashioned RFID, but it will work." He tapped the gun's nose against the side of the ship behind which we hid. "The rest of the rounds in here are tranq."

"I could use one," I said.

There was the dull *plunk* of an air gun followed by the explosion of a round lobbed through the air. The thug pulled his leather jacket over both of us. "Fuck," he said. I agreed with him.

A gelatin capsule exploded and screams of fear gave way to shrieks of agony. I smelled skin turning to jelly, and realized only too late that my body wasn't completely concealed under the jacket.

I thanked god that the nerves in my left arm hadn't been turned on, or the pain would have been unbearable. The *thunk-plunk* point and counterpoint rang out again, the shell flying out of the tube followed by a *whoosh* of flame and napalm fed by oxygen searing through flesh. After the whisper sound of the scorching came barely human howls.

The man next to me was speaking quietly, and it was only after he threw his jacket off that I realized he had been counting how many shots Matthew had fired. He ran out into the open like he was also probably counting how much time he had to hit Immer with the tranq dart before the killer reloaded and he got scorched bad enough to wish he'd been hit with a bullet.

I stood and looked at the aluminum and steel basket framework of my arm, bits of melted silicone flesh and grafted gristle dripping like congealed fat into puddles on the ground. There was too much real flesh burning for anyone to pay attention to me, although the screams and moans were drowned out as thrusters came to life again and the other Air Fox took to the skies.

The thug looked up at the aircraft moving in a vertical line toward the clouds. He didn't appear to discourage by the killer's escape, but then again he'd shot the guy successfully with a tracker.

"You coming?" he asked, motioning with his cinderblock head toward the open gullwing doors of the remaining bird. The med techs were in worse shape than my arm, lying sprawled out and burnt on the ground.

"I'm not doing a hotlink on a Fedgov bird."

"You should really turn your subvoc to your scanner sometime." He holstered his Needlegun. "Aren't you a former cop?"

He walked toward the driver's side of the bird. I followed him, not because I was thinking about going with him but because I was confused. "What the hell are you talking about?"

I heard his subvoc to override the retinal scan on the Air Fox. "Identity confirmed," the onboard computer said. He looked at me. "You're wanted for a double murder at the Ming. You left enough DNA to start a sperm bank."

My heart fell to my feet. "Well, in that case." I walked around to the other side of the bird and sat in the passenger seat. Its contoured leather was climate-controlled, cool water running through its ribbed form on this humid night.

"You got to get rid of that cyber arm, though."

I looked down at the metallic remains of my arm, two vestigial fingers writhing around myomar plastic muscles. Spasms wracked what was left of the limb. "I can't control it," I said.

"That's why you got to dump it." He fixed me with his cold Slavic eyes. "If it doesn't have a fast catch, then I'll blow it off for you at the joint. But I don't want a haywire limb anywhere near an instrument panel, not while I'm in the air."

"It's got a catch," I said. I was afraid to touch the steaming limb, and so hopped out of the bird and subvoc'd a "Release" command. The arm dropped to the ground, where scattered real limbs already lay in charred blackened piles. I got back in the bird after ditching the arm.

The doors closed like retracting batwings and my partner laughed as we took off. "They don't like me much in this Node. Last time I was here I took some teeth out and I ain't exactly a dentist."

I was thankful to have my Babel mod functioning, since he had a capital sense of humor and I didn't want to miss anything. The ship was aloft, floating toward white volutes of cloud that looked like smoke blown from the lungs of a sky god. "Where are we going?"

"ER," he subvoc'd as we split the clouds and studied a readout from his wristband as he flew. "Looks like we're heading south."

My stomach somersaulted again. I was wanted for murder and my only option was to go beyond the safety of Schengen walls toward a killer hiding in the Edge. At least if we kept heading south that was where we would end up.

"We've never really met under auspicious circumstances," I said. He looked over at me. Whatever languages he knew, he didn't know "auspicious" even in his native tongue. I tried again. "I don't even know your name, even though I know we've met. If you're going to cover my six going in, I at least need something to call you."

His Cro-Magnon jaw pulsed as he mulled that over. "You are right," he said. "Ruslan." Pleasantries had been dispensed. "You packing?"

I pulled out the diamond poker. It was a wonder I hadn't impaled myself in all the commotion.

"Better than nothing," Ruslan said. "But you kill him, I have to kill you." He shrugged. "Boss's orders."

"I understand."

"So far, you haven't fucked with us so we won't fuck with you."

"Reciprocity's a fundamental rule of human nature."

He either ignored or didn't understand what I said. "Look out there," he said.

"Oh, shit!"

I looked through the clear front hull of the Air Fox, toward the wall separating Schengen from the Edge. The dividing wall was smooth and stone, curved at the lip like a cooling tower. Surface to air MANPADs appeared from their hideaways in the wall and aimed toward us.

It was standard procedure to fire onto any aircraft not cleared to enter Schengen, but if they knew a Fedgov craft was jacked they wouldn't hesitate to blow us out of the sky even though we were exiting. "Hold on." Ruslan pulled back on the Y-flipped controls and I couldn't escape the feeling that my balls were flying into my brain as we rushed upward at a steep angle.

I closed my eyes, breathed in, and then exhaled in shivering spasms. Ruslan tagged me on the chest with his right hand. "You scared of flying?"

"No, I'm scared of surface-to-air missiles." He laughed at that.

"We're clear," he said. He was still splitting his eyeballs between the airspace ahead and the ER in his peripherals. I admired his multitasking, but I didn't like distracted flyers or psychopathic ones. I understood he was loyal to his boss, but every time I made eye contact with him I couldn't ignore the murderous glint or the set of the jaw that left me with the impression he might nosedive and pull a kamikaze maneuver.

I looked down. "Holy shit." I gazed on the burnt remains of a Leviathan drone. Now that it was downed it looked like a massive stingray that had been bitten in half by a great white shark. "I've never seen one of those shot down."

"That's how you know it's bad." We made a steep incline back into the clouds. "Why do you think I'm flying higher?" he asked.

I wasn't a total gearhead, but I was well-acquainted with that model of mega-drone. It had a persistent stare function equivalent to a hundred of its smaller brethren. Its wingspan was one-hundred and thirty feet, and back in the Nodes it could have stayed airborne for two days at sixty-thousand feet. It hadn't managed to float for a thousand meters in the Edge.

"Stay loose, Detective." Ruslan gave me another one of his love taps, and then returned his hand to the chore of steering. We did a few more evasive maneuvers, or what passed for such in this lumbering craft. Then we drifted lower again.

"Can this thing shoot back?" I wondered what we would do if a stinger or other SAM flew toward us. I doubted the Edge had the kind of firepower of the Schengen's wall guard, but RPGs were probably easier to find here than potable water.

"She's got belly mounted miniguns. I can override them out of their pods, if you want to try firing them."

I thought about it. Rus spoke before I could answer. "We're close to him."

"You mean we're gaining on him?"

"No. He's stopped moving."

I gripped my icepick in my right hand. It was a terrible feeling to have a knife I might need and to know that if I used it to save my life Ruslan would be there to blow my head off. I didn't have many options, and the ones I had were bad. If I couldn't prove that Matthew Immer had killed Tia Mifune, Kyra Boxer, and Viva Jasmine, then I was toast.

"Look alive," Ruslan said. We were descending so that I could now make out the long, wending towpath that had been beaten by the feet of refugees fleeing toward Schengen City. "Want to take the snake somewhere?"

I didn't get his joke, until my eye drifted from the towpath to a gargantuan junkyard where old model discarded maglev snakes apparently went to die. Citizens of this outland had joined the train cars together into a kind of bowery of rusted metalwork linked and shoved into the configuration of a city.

"I didn't know people actually tried to live in this rattrap," Ruslan said.

"That took some work, but it looks abandoned."

Ruslan squinted as he checked something on his ER. "Population density of twelve-hundred people per acre."

"Jesus."

"I think even Jesus forgot about this place, comrade." The bay of the Air Fox opened, and landing gear deployed. "This is it."

The big-bellied Medivac vehicle was getting ready to land in among a cluster of buildings. They were so old and desiccated they didn't look like a ghetto, but more like the ruins of an ancient civilization. A couple of buildings had even been taken over by ivy, completing the impression. Wheels touched down on the roof and Ruslan triggered the rig's arrestors.

We came to a halt. I held the dagger in my one remaining hand. "What now?" I asked.

"Now we put this bastard to sleep, bring him to Mr. Timofev, and ask him the recipe for that one little cake he bakes so well."

"I need to clear my name."

He held up a hand, reaching into his jacket for the Needlegun again. "We get this guy back to Timofev, we ask him what he knows. He doesn't tell us, we send his little piggies to market, hook his balls to alligator clips, and put a pain mod on him. Then we increase the threshold until his eyeballs bleed. After that he will tell us."

"And then, for me?"

"We give you reconstruction, a fingerprint graft, and then send you to the Amero zone. Maybe you like the Mexican coast. They've had a big recovery I heard."

"Okay." Tequila in cantinas and sun on the white sands beat death.

The gullwing doors eased open, and Ruslan hopped out. Gravel crunched underfoot. He whispered, "Be on the lookout for traps. Do you have a mod?"

"Yeah," I said. "Denholm, I need eyes."

"Sir, the roof is unstable."

That was a comment rather than a second set of eyes, but he must have known what he was talking about. It was probably a combination of the Air Fox's weight along with the general vagaries of time and decay. Whatever it was, the roof of the building pulled inward like a sinkhole or water swirling around a drain. Ruslan and I ran for the sturdier eaves and edge of the mansard roof. I grabbed the stone wings of a gargoyle statue and held on.

We were at the rim of a new hole formed in the center of the roof. The dust settled and we started walking forward to inspect the pit's yawning mouth as carefully as kids skating on a lake of thin ice. Below us was the main room of an old art deco theater, the burgundy curtains moth-eaten and the mosaic tiled walls chipped so that the unpolished terrazzo hieroglyphs couldn't be deciphered

I wasn't sure how we were going to get down. It was safe to assume that Matthew Immer knew we were in his lair even if he didn't have any tripwires or sensors about. If we hadn't lost the element of surprise when we touched down, we had when we'd wrecked the roof. Any ropes or cords that might let us rappel downward were lost with our aircraft. I knew people with mods for hideaway ropes and grapples on their bodies, but I wasn't one of them.

I turned to Ruslan "Any ideas, Rus?"

His face was expressionless. "We jump."

CHAPTER NINETEEN

IN THE BELLY OF THE EGG MAN

A math problem was barely audible coming from Ruslan's subvoc. My new friend did not look much like a math whiz, and I wondered what he was doing.

"Come here," he said, barely audible. He didn't waste any more time talking. He pulled me to his front and had me hold him around the throat. "Lock your legs around my waist," he said. I wasn't the most homophobic guy in the world, but I hesitated.

Ruslan spoke through clenched teeth. "I just did a force calculation on my Yamakasi mod." He looked down into the hole in the roof, where the Air Fox had plunged nosecone first. "We can make the jump, but you have to be holding me."

"Alright." I curled up to him with my one remaining arm, like a baby koala on its mother's front. I heard a mass times acceleration figure work through his head, and I closed my eyes as he ran around the edges of the roof where it hadn't collapsed.

"Why do you even have a Yamakasi mod?" I asked. He didn't strike me as someone interested in gymnastics or interpretive dance.

"Remember when we were flying through here the other day and we saw that guy doing parkour on the fire escape?"

I thought back to my ride with him and his boss. "Yeah," I said. "I remember."

"I was never into that, but I did have to teach soldiers how to navigate obstacle courses back when I was training them to fight Chechens."

"Makes sense."

He stepped lively as if doing tire drills and then zagged left and ran until he reached the mouth of the crater. He swept left, tuck-rolling as we fell. He held me to his chest as we tumbled onto the torn carpet of the theater's floor. We had made it. I looked around.

There were sconce lights on the wall, their cases shaped like half-shells. They glowed with what I thought was candlepower. Closer inspection revealed it to be electric light. The Edge was not supposed to be juiced, although there were rumors of bootleg hookups siphoning energy from the Schengen.

Ruslan stepped lively around the downed aircraft, bits of glass from a fallen chandelier crunching under his black boots. Shards of champagne-colored baubles glowed, while the zinc point of the art nouveau ceiling fixture pierced the ground of the auditorium like the point of a javelin.

A beam of light shot downward and we both hit the deck, hiding in among chairs whose vinyl seat cushions were ripped and leaking upholstery.

Ruslan whispered something to me, but I couldn't hear his words. He stood and spoke again. "It's a projector."

I stood with him, followed the white light beam from the projector's booth down to the canvas of the ripped screen. An old eight-millimeter hygiene film played on what was left of the shredded cloth. A gloved hand dragged a scalpel across a pregnant woman's belly and made to pull a baby through the slit of a Caesarian section. I turned away from the bloody tableau.

A shadow passed before the entrance to the theater, and we both turned and started running up the sloped floor. Ruslan looked down at his RFID wrist piece and I pulled my crystal knife from inside of my jacket. He shook his tranq gun at me. "Let me put him to sleep, or I'll put you in a coffin."

"Okay."

We burst through the door, into a lobby that smelled of rancid popcorn butter. The floor was pocked with cigarette burns that ruined the effect of the lilies patterned on the carpet. Whoever'd rigged up power for the lights and the hygiene film had also started on wiring the concession, too. A hotdog roller grill was rotating, stained with grease. There were no hotdogs in sight, and I shuddered to think what kind of meat might have been cooked there or would be grilled there in the future.

The shadow was punctuated by a shout this time, both the sound and light coming from our left in the direction of another screening room in the movie palace. Ruslan ran ahead of me and I let him. He pushed open the door to the theater and put his Parkour program to work. He rolled left as the airy report of another paintball was followed by the sizzle of a gelatin cap exploding on the far wall of the theater. The acid of the capsule melted through stone with a crackle.

The killer ducked behind the front row of seats, and fired unseen. He popped shots on an arc, like a mortar man. I crouched low and walked alongside the right wall upholstered in claret-covered velvet. I prayed to god the killer was focused on Ruslan, and that I could blindside him from the right. There was another lazy *plunk* followed by a noise that made every hair on my right arm stand up straight.

"Kill him," Ruslan shouted. "Fuck the boss!" He must have been burning pretty bad to defy Timofev's orders. At the same time, I feared he might have given away my position with his shouts.

There was no time to hesitate, or even think. I turned left when I made it to the front of the seating area. I prepared to rush forward and stab the living shit out of Mr. Immer with my icepick. I had to get him or he was going to melt both of our asses with that paintball gun.

Any sane man would have been loath to discharge that piece at such close range, since the risk of splash back meant hitting me would carry the risk that he'd also burn himself. I knew I was dealing with a madman though.

I didn't know how crazy he was until I was upon him. He lay in a pile, looking up at the ceiling. The gun had left his hand, and he was smiling. Ruslan was silent. "You're too late," the killer said.

"Fuck you." I dropped the knife from my right hand and grabbed his collar. I picked his head up, gathering locks of his hair that had been permanently dyed white by the decontamination showers in Tmu Tarakan.

I slammed his head against the hard floor of the theater. It made me feel better, so I did it again. "Fuck you," I repeated, still angry.

"Too late." His eyes bulged from their sockets, as if he had Graves' disease or his head was a balloon someone had overinflated.

My subvoc was still turned on, and I had caught the echo of his command to initiate his body's hemlock mod. His heartrate was slowing and he was dying. That should have been enough to satisfy me, but the problem was that he wasn't dying painfully.

That nightmare scream rang out again, the same one that had led us into this theater. I knew it wasn't Ruslan. He was dead. The shout came again, only this time it was accompanied by the voices of whining babies.

The killer looked up at me, smiling. "They want milk."

I punched him in the nose with my right hand. Blood leaked from his nostrils, down into his smiling mouth. The canvas of the screen was ripped apart as two crawling babies like the one I'd seen at The Ming pushed their way through the cloak separating one level of hell from a deeper ring.

One of the babies wore a soft faux panda outfit with a hoodie shaped to look like bear ears. The other baby was naked. He didn't even wear a diaper. He cooed as he shuffled forward, his anatomically correct tiny penis the size of a martini olive or an adult's outie bellybutton.

"Mommy!" They said in unison. I knew what was coming and I lifted the broken and suicidal bastard in my arms, and held him up in front of me like a human shield. The guns buried beneath the heads of the babies discharged their first shells, blowing through the ceramic skulls of the infant dolls. The rest of the lead poured into the body of the man I held, who flopped like a fish and danced until the bullets ran out.

Smoke wafted into the air, and the baby-gun hybrids collapsed to the floor. "Thank you." The man who had been screaming now spoke calmly. I dropped the dead body in my arms, and lifted myself onto the wooden stage apron before the torn and tattered screen canvas.

I could see the face of the man before me. He had ancient features, a hatchet nose and a sloping forehead. Like most people I couldn't shake the silly notion that a big head meant a big brain. It wasn't just the forehead that gave his face the look of intelligence, however. It was the dark eyes, the shadowy glower and the pursed lips. He'd looked much meaner in the previous images I'd seen of him. Bernard Blankstone now looked humbled by the ordeal he'd endured.

I walked toward him. It was dark in there, since fewer of the sconce lights on the wall were functioning in this theater than in the last one. That made it harder to see whatever was wrapped around his body, concealing everything except for the face. He was entombed in the wall, with all below his head invisible in some sort of blanketing cocoon. The mummifying layer smelled like green manure. It made moist suctioning sounds, like a tar pit burbling as it swallowed a creature that accidentally stumbled into its mire.

"What the hell is going on?"

"Light switch is on the far wall."

I ran to the wall, and felt around. He spoke from behind me as he struggled. "He manufactured a pretty good vat-grown simulacrum of me."

"Why?"

"He tried to blackmail me. I wouldn't pay."

So far my hand hadn't hit any light switch. I finally felt the nub of a switch and flipped the toggle. Nothing happened. "Lights are out," I said.

"Shit," he grunted. "Kyra refused to go along. She warned me, and the next thing I know I was kidnapped. I woke up here. How is she by the way? I know he said he stung her first."

I didn't want to tell him that she was dead, or that I was suspected of her murder. I was about to ask him what he meant by saying she was "stung." There was the groan of a power surge, and the house lights flooded on. "Jesus Christ, god in heaven," I said.

My mouth was open enough for an army of ants to march right on in. To the left of Bernard Blankstone was a glass tank enclosure, a tissue vat like the one where the constituents for my own left arm had been grown. What must have been a dozen free floating female breasts bounced on Jacuzzi jets, swimming in collagen saccharide. "Need a pair?" Bernard asked.

There was a workbench in front of the tank, like the one that Lazlo the Toymaker kept in his shop. On the table was what looked like a massive stinger from a gargantuan hornet. Blankstone saw my gaze fixed on the thing. My mouth was still open and he knew I probably wouldn't get around to asking him what it was, so he answered my unasked question. "It's not a gun. It's an ovipositor."

"What's in it?"

"It's what he shot into the women's breasts, and into me."

I turned to look at him, which was a mistake. His body was encased in what looked like a numberless swarm of maggots that were segmented like worms. They had woven into one giant encasement wrapped around him tightly. Bits of his skin were visible, although even what was once him had also evidently been colonized. His skin was infected, dry and cracked. His epidermis was red and irritated, as if something had burrowed through the tissue, fed and laid eggs. When my gaze reached his crotch, I saw an outpouring of something like confetti or Chinese vermicelli noodles. They were squirming to break free like living wet spaghetti wending through holes in the colander they had made of his groin by punching their way outward.

"It castrated me," he said, explaining the absent genitals. "I need you to kill me."

"You don't have a hemlock?"

He groaned again. "No, you can't have a hemlock and be chief executive of a hotdog stand. It's apparently a sign of weak leadership abilities. If you're the kind of guy who's willing to even consider suicide, I guess they think that means the competition will eat your lunch." He shook his head to the extent the web around him would allow. "The Japanese had seppuku. The Romans could fall on their swords." Bernard chuckled slightly. "I guess I just drank milk from the wrong breast."

I held up my diamond sticker. "This is all I have."

He blinked patiently, pursed his lips, and nodded. "That'll do. I can assure you I'm in tremendous pain, and death would be an improvement."

"I could cut you out," I offered. "Free you, get you a Medivac."

"No," he said. "I'm not going home without my dick and my balls. Let me die with the little bit of dignity I have intact." His voice was low, pleading. "Please."

"Okay," I said, and dropped the knife.

I walked back through the torn canvas, over to Ruslan's steaming prone form. His tranq gun had welded to his flesh. He was napalmed into one waxen pile of meat, bone, and metal. The minigun was made of stern stuff and hadn't melted. It was holstered in one of two utility slots in a rig that had flown free from his scorched body at some point in the shootout. I took the gun out and walked back in the direction of the stage.

"Found something better?" he asked.

"This should be less painful," I said, standing before him.

"I appreciate this."

"Sure."

I pointed the gun at him. He closed his eyes and whispered, "I lift my eyes up to the mountain." I wasn't religious and my Babel kept me from knowing for sure what language he was speaking, but I hazarded he was reciting some Hebrew death prayer. I squeezed the trigger of the hand cannon, which wasn't hard since it was filed down to a fine hair. I aimed for his head.

There was the gaseous whine of the gun heating up, and a full Gatling-style rotation followed. There was a wet pop and his head burst into what looked like a blasting spray of postmodern art that painted the wall behind him. I dropped the piece and walked backwards until I almost fell off the stage.

Whatever kind of parasite Matthew Immer had injected into him with the ovipositor sounded as if it was now stirring in the dead billionaire's bowels. There was a rumble like diarrhea as the parasite sensed the host was dead and it needed a new home. I wasn't leasing space in my own body. I turned on a dime and rushed up the sloping steps of the nightmare theater I was sure would haunt me in my dreams for a long time to come.

The door burst open just as I was running for it. Detective Dear and a group of SPD extraction crew appeared. The men were faceless behind riot helmets and bulky with padding and Kevlar.

"Run!" I shouted. "The bomb's set to blow!"

They turned around and ran, and I hauled ass with them. I followed behind them so fast that I was soon out in front, coming to the room where the Air Fox was planted and half-shattered. It was so shellacked with debris and bits and pieces of rock that it was easy to believe it had been lodged in the ground for years, maybe even centuries. It reminded me a bit of that vintage theme restaurant in the Casino Node, where the front of the building was done up to make it seem like a Chevy Malibu had collided with the restaurant so hard that only the taillights, massive chrome bumper, and fins were visible from the façade.

This crew had at least thought to bring belaying ropes with them, for which I was grateful. I shimmied upward with them, climbing the nylon ties hand-over fist until we reached the rubbly edge of the roof where hovercraft waited.

"You're lucky that Rusky wasn't the only one monitoring Immer." Lieutenant Dear pointed toward the nearest SPD extractor. "Get in," he said, "and maybe you can tell me on our ride back to Schengen City why I shouldn't charge you with triple homicide."

I slid into the vehicle. "I'll do my best," I said, which wasn't the whole truth since I had started out by lying to them about a bomb about to go off in the movie palace. The hell of it was that if I had said a parasite was about to hatch, I was afraid that might not give them a sense of urgency. It might have made them more curious to get a look at what was going on behind the curtain in that dim theater.

We were evacuating out of there, lifting off and soaring away so quickly that we would be long gone before whatever hatched from Bernard Blankstone escaped and went sliming its way around the Edge. If it needed to find a live mammalian body shortly after the death of its present host, then I thought Schengen City had a chance to survive. If it could live on its own and slink around until it found another body, then we were in trouble. We were doomed if it discovered a way to reach nursing mothers and transferred its own DNA to the suckling babes.

I tried not to think about it on our ride back over the wall into the glowing city. I was happy to see the glass-skinned skyscrapers, the neon pulsing and the searchlights crossing streams with one another as they poisoned the clouds above.

Dear tapped me where my left arm had once been as we flew toward Schengen Med Central. "You forgot something in the Green Node."

"I'll get another arm," I said. The only problem was that I couldn't get another mind, not without losing the good memories with the bad. Truth be told however, I had a hell of a lot more bad memories than good. But who didn't?

CHAPTER TWENTY

ARMED AGAINST PAIN

The shower was set to Tropical Storm mode, and Denholm even sprinkled in some screeching howler monkeys and a toucan song to add to the effect. I looked up at the ceiling-mounted brushed steel plate and opened my mouth to drink in the faux dew.

"Sir, your guest's ETA is now ten minutes."

"Thank you, Denholm." I sent a signal to kill the water, and a final drip pelted my back as I wiped the fogged glass with my hand. I stepped out of the shower and lifted my arms. The hideaway blowers appeared from the tiled walls and hit me with blasts of warm air.

I looked down at my left arm. Denholm must have been piggybacking on my vision since he asked, "How is your new arm working, sir?"

"Good," I said, "although we're about to see how good."

I slipped on my brown terrycloth robe and tied the front as I stepped out of the bathroom. The lights turned off behind me automatically. My butler stood there in black tie and white gloves, holding breakfast on a tray. Room service had come while I was showering, but I'd programmed Denholm to let them in. It was maybe an oversight on my part, since I probably still had enemies willing to kill me who wouldn't mind stooping to pose as room service to plant a slug in my brain.

Denholm eased my concern as he handed me over my breakfast. "Sir, I've been perusing the scream feeds while you've been showering."

"Yes?" I took my breakfast, the South of the Border special. It was a wrap filled with scrambled eggs, hash browns, and pepper jack cheese. The steam from the omelet made my mouth water before I'd even put a fork to it. I started chewing the tortilla, and spoke to Denholm while a globule of sour cream was still on my tongue. "Give me some good news."

"Verbatim from the screamer or should I summarize?"

I gulped down some egg and then chased that with cold OJ. I burped and said, "Summarize. I trust you." Even when things had been most haywire in the Nodes, no one had bothered to commandeer Denholm. I was sure that probably had more to do with his antivirus software, but I liked to believe it was also because he was loyal. I had to believe that because otherwise I had no friends.

"A warehouse in the Muscovite District was shut down, after an anonymous source revealed that additive manufacturers had been reprogrammed to make everything from fake Gucci purses and Prada shoes to knockoff Cartier watches."

"Go on." I thought I knew where this was going, but I let him continue.

"Captain William Dear, formerly Lieutenant and lately promoted for his work on the Blankstone murder, says that the new ultra-high resolution scanning on the machines seized makes him suspect internal espionage as well as counterfeiting. Multiple designer firms were believed to have had their patent ingredient lists compromised by-"

I held up my hand. "Wait, wait. Let me guess, a Russian or maybe a Kazak."

"Very good sir."

That explained why Vasily Timofev hadn't decided to kill me. He didn't bother to do as much as put out a lowball contract on me, even though I'd failed to bring him Matthew Immer alive. I'd also probably helped contribute to getting his flunky burned to death in the process by not moving fast enough.

I doubted the kingpin gave two shits about the death of his foot soldier, although I knew he was desperate to get that recipe for the new synthesized opiate. *C'est la Vie.* "What are you going to do?" I asked Denholm.

"Sir, what would you like me to do?"

"It's a rhetorical question, my good man."

"I see."

It was a load off my mind. I'd first cleared my name by taking a full P300 battery at the Schengen Dungeon. They'd poked, prodded, and checked to establish that I had no mods that would allow me to spoof an EKG or MRI. They'd found no implants to give me the sociopath's edge, and all their eggheads had gone through my cerebral cortex with the computational equivalent of a fine-toothed comb. They'd probed with a PET scan, showing me crime scene photos of the three women in question. They'd watched the color positron emissions for the telltale signs of that "brain on fire," those cauliflower hemispheres and regions lighting orange or glowing red.

The images of the slain women disturbed me, but didn't betray me as a liar to the mind molesters in white lab coats as they studiously ignored my whimpering while scribbling on their clipboards.

Lieutenant Dear had been courteous to me the whole time. He apologized, brought coffee, and glazed crullers whenever the inquisition entered a new phase. The last test included a forensic phonetician, who placed the sticky sides of electrodes against my naked chest and clipped my finger inside of a heartrate monitor.

I'd answered their questions, and then they'd transferred me to a Fedgov butcher shop where they fitted me with a new arm. It was only after I had regained consciousness after the operation that I'd been told I was no longer a person of interest, and that I could go back to my life as house detective at the Zhakpot.

And that was what I did.

A knock came at the door. It was an old-fashioned rapping of knuckles even though Mary and I had established a subvoc link after I touched base with her. I flipped open the tray on my new arm and entered the code the doc had given me to release Oxycodone when the pain hit.

I was supposed to press the drip switch whenever I felt a burn in my joints where the new arm had been linked, but I was abusing the drug to deal with my fear of the woman at the door. I hadn't touched a woman in years, at least not like this.

"Coming." I walked softly to the door and peeked through the keyhole. There she was. Mary Sitzmann had butternut skin and mahogany hair so rich it tinted toward purple. Her smile was wide, natural, and something about the crooked set of her imperfect teeth made her even more sexy than she looked in the image of her on the ad listing her as the new CEO of Touch LLC.

"Hello." I opened the door and stood aside for her.

"Hey."

I held out my right hand for a shake, and she held both of her arms open for a hug. I tried that, widening my arms like a high-schooler awkwardly slow dancing for the first time. I didn't know where I would rest my hands once I got my arms around her. She was small, and her diminutive frame disappeared in my bear arms. I feared her and what she might think of me.

She placed her hands against my spine, and rubbed the columns of my backbone through the fabric of the bathrobe. Part of what I was feeling was the first effects of the time-release opiate, but some of it was her fingers. Most of it was her fingers.

Mary Sitzmann hugged me tightly until my arms were flat against my sides, with my hands turned inward and thumbs where the seams of my pants would be if I'd been wearing pants.

We both let go of one another, and I was relieved to see I didn't have an erection. I didn't want to come off as a pig, and the truth was I needed affection more than sex. Too much had happened and my nerves were shot. It felt as if every cell in my body was a termite that had turned on its wooden host.

My eyes watered as I felt something thaw. I didn't want to cry and break a thirty-year streak of stoicism, but I was close. She looked up, so much smaller than me and yet so much stronger. She grazed me slightly with her nails and it felt like morphine. I batted my eyes and a damn tear escaped from my right eye, betraying me.

"Let's go over to the bed," she said.

"Okay."

I preceded her over there. I lay on my left side, looking out the window. I was terrified just to let her touch me. To look her in the eyes while crying would have been too much. I felt her sink into the bed behind me. It was an all-but imperceptible shift in weight as she settled in, since she was so light. I looked out toward the emerald Statue of Liberty, holding its torch aloft between a steel-clad Giza pyramid clone and an Eifel Tower. The tower looked a little bit too much like a giant version of that ovipositor tool I saw in my dreams. It was the one that had cocooned Blankstone and poisoned the women, the one wielded by the man I wished was alive again just so that I could kill him once more.

"Relax," she said, her fingers alternately tickling and scratching my back. I wanted my anger and hate, because they were a large part of what kept me going. Her fingers were taking that away from me, and it felt too good for me to be angry with her for robbing me of my defenses. I was doubly glad now that I didn't have to look at her, because I was smiling for the first time in years. I thought that somehow letting her see me smile would be even worse than letting her see me cry.

"Good," she said, "in through the nose, out through the mouth."

I obeyed as best I could, shivering a bit as I did. Her voice was so serene in timbre I didn't know if she was speaking or subvoc'ing. "I wish I'd known they were so pet-friendly here."

"Yeah," I shivered from her touch as it converted my nerves from enemies to friends. I wondered if everyone else's mind, body, and spirit were always fighting against them. Or maybe it was me doing the fighting.

"I could have brought Luna."

"Luna?" I was feeling too drowsy, sated from breakfast, drugs, and her touch to form a full sentence without taking extra pains.

"My mini-shepherd."

Her tickling fingers danced from the nape of my neck to the small of my back. I continued crying, although silently. She must have heard it or somehow still known, because her voice whispered, "It's okay. It's okay."

It was okay. The problem was that it couldn't remain so. That was the trouble with drugs, with women, with life. We shouldn't have been able to touch something without being able to grasp it I thought, unless they were going to allow us to keep it, whoever they were.

"Remind me to call down after you go," I said, "and I'll get your dog a bandana with the Zhakpot logo on it."

"Luna will love that! Thank you."

She tapped me on the shoulder with the hand that had previously been tickling, stroking, massaging.

"It's okay," she said, and just like that the voices that had been eating me up for years finally quieted. She had killed an army with her tiny fingers.

"Can she come here to eat?" she asked.

I assumed we were still talking about Luna. "She can eat in any restaurant that has a patio area. She just can't come onto the gaming floor unless she has a discipline mod."

"I don't believe in those," she said. "I've heard they're cruel, that they hurt the dogs when the dogs try to defy them."

"Could be," I said. I'd never had a dog or a pet of any kind, but maybe now was the time to get one.

She stopped stroking me. "What did you just release?"

"What?"

"You forget, we were subvoc linked after you called me so I can see the command. It's encrypted, but I recognize the first three letters in the code as a time-release cipher."

Mary was a smart woman. "You're right. It's a synth opioid. I did it because my nerves were driving me crazy. I wasn't sure if I could meet you."

Her feet snaked around the front of my body, the wrinkled soles and balls of her own feet locking over the tops of mine. I swallowed a mouthful of saliva and trembled slightly. In through the nose, out through the mouth. She seemed to revel in the power she had, although there was no cruelty in her dominance. There was just pleasure that as a tiny Elvin creature with dark hair, soft skin, and deep eyes she knew she was somehow still more powerful than a violence-prone ex-cop.

"Are you happy I'm here?"

"Yes."

I couldn't fight the erection, although at least the tears had stopped. She touched my earlobes and stroked them with her fingers so delicately that my body went limp. She held me close, as if it was possible for me to fall through space if I got free from her grip even though we were safe together in bed.

"You don't need exogenous dope," she said, and it was hard for me to follow the thread of her words. I was incapacitated by comfort, pleasure, and something so safe I confused it for love even though I knew it wasn't and couldn't be. "Your body produces natural endorphins when you get touched." Mary let her fingers drift from my ears and she started massaging my neck, a traditional Swedish release grip that sapped the stress from me.

"Your body will produce opiate alkaloids if it's touched right."

I believed her. I was pretty sure that was what my body was doing right then, although I also thought there was a chance that I was getting a boost from the drip I'd programmed before she entered my suite.

"Sir."

Denholm's voice made her spring up so fast I almost got bounced off the bed. "Oh my god!" She placed her dainty hand over her sternum. "He freaked me out so much."

"He should," I said. "He was narrow AI, but he's been reprogrammed as strong."

She walked toward him. "What does he want?"

"He can speak for himself," I said, and then Denholm did just that. "Sir, I would like to excuse myself, perhaps go to the lobby and allow you two some privacy."

Mary pushed some of her black hair behind her pixyish ear. "I'm not a prostitute," she said.

"I understand that, Madame," Denholm said.

I shook myself from my ecstatic stupor, and walked like a drunken man until I was between them. I gripped the front of my terrycloth robe to keep my erection from popping out.

"Calm down," I said, to both or either of them. Denholm looked readier to listen to reason, but I knew little about women and nothing about how to placate them when they were mad. I knew enough from experience to know my efforts would probably only make her madder.

Lucky enough for me she calmed down on her own. "He wants to leave," I said, "because he perceives this as intimate." I thought back to what Tia Mifune said. "It's not sexual, but it is sensual. I've spent enough time with him for him to develop a..." I faltered.

"Conscience?" she asked. The raven hair she'd tucked behind her ear fell free and framed her narrow-pointed jaw.

"Something like that," I said. It wasn't my intention to creep her out, and I hoped my next gesture didn't do that but rather distracted her enough to admire rather than fear the machine-man in her midst.

I placed my hand on the top of his head and gave two turns. I removed the skullcap and revealed the microprocessors and grids of streaking light patterns that were ice-blue and laser-green channels coursing like neon maglevs in some tiny futuristic city. The trick worked. The light reflected in the perfect skin of her dark face.

"There is a full human neocortex translated into code in here," I said.

She held her hand out, debating whether to touch the glass-encased bubble. Mary beamed.

"A neuron makes about ten-thousand connections to neighboring neurons." The spiel I recited was directly from the engineer who'd done the tweaking. "There are billions of neurons in the brain, which means there are as many connections in a cubic centimeter of Denholm's brain as there are stars in the Milky Way galaxy."

"Amazing ..."

She reached her gentle hand forward and touched him lightly under the chin. I sensed a slight twitch in him. Mary must have noticed it too, for she drew back as if afraid she had activated his self-destruct chip by introducing him to female touch.

I replaced the top of his head. "Now you see why he wants to leave us in peace. He understands it's personal, and not sexual."

Her fingers drifted toward my eyes, and she wiped a tear away. Not only had Denholm never seen me cry, no woman had ever seen me cry. Not even my wife.

"Okay," she said, calming now that she knew she wasn't being insulted as a prostitute. Denholm clicked the heels of his black shoes and turned away from us, walking toward the door.

Her saucer eyes glowed as she looked up at me. She held her palm out toward the bed. "Shall we resume?"

"Let's."

I moved to the right half of the bed, and shuffled until I was on the edge. I felt her warmth behind me, and her soft breath touched my shoulder. "Are you comfortable like that?"

"Yes."

"You can take off your robe," she said. "I feel comfortable with you being naked, if you do."

"No," I said. "It's okay."

She eased toward me in the bed, threw her feet back over me, and did her best to resume the posture and mood that had been set before Denholm had spoken. "So how did you hear about us?"

Lies would work better than truth in this instance. I'd been a person of interest and then a flat-out suspect in the Blankstone case, but my name had stayed out of the screamers. She wouldn't know that Tia Mifune had been one of my clients, a client who I had failed.

I decided to lie. "I just put Denholm on the task. I told him to start with massage and go from there."

"Now I know you weren't lying about how smart your butler friend is." He'd left the room already, closing the door behind him. "He definitely didn't steer you wrong."

"Did you found Touch?" I asked, doubling down on my deceit.

"No," she said, her voice untouched by a trace of suspicion or at least not showing it. "The founder had an accident, and I took over for her. A couple of us girls bought part ownership, anyway."

"Oh."

"Okay," she said. Her tone had changed and we were clearly getting down to the core of the ritual. "This is a position I call the laying runner. This will work best, since you seem vulnerable right now. I think we're going to maintain this one for the rest of the session. Next time we'll try something else."

That made me flush and glow, the idea that I would see her again and that I would feel her again. "Alright."

Her feet wrapped tighter around my own, and her arms slinked over my shoulder. I couldn't escape the impossible feeling that she was growing and I was shrinking, or the idea that she had been larger than me from the very beginning.

I didn't fight the shrinking feeling. I felt comfortable and instinctively curled up. That must have been what she wanted, for she whispered "Good" and I shivered again. She spoke or subvoc'd, and I listened. I let her voice travel through me and carry me as I closed my eyes and moved through a blackness that didn't scare me.

"I'm sure you've heard of a runner's high. It releases a bunch of endorphins, chief among them beta endorphin. This," she said, "is a natural opiate that accompanies pregnancy right until after birth is completed. Having a baby made me a much better cuddler than I'd been before I was a mother."

I curled into a tighter ball. I tucked my knees to my elbows without knowing what I was doing, as if reverse gestating and going from fetal position to something even more embryonic. I felt powerless, eyeless, mouthless, earless, but it wasn't a problem since I no longer needed my senses to protect me. Mary was all around me, curling tighter and growing larger as I spiraled further in on myself like a Fibonacci curl, a maze made of one man.

"No one knows for sure," the voice said, above and around me, "but the fetus could be floating around with its own opiate receptors loaded with those endorphins. The baby might be getting high just as the mother's getting high."

I opened my eyes and floated through warm salty water, cocooned in a red veined pouch with tight soft walls closing in around me. The ecstasy that had been poached from me at birth was back. I didn't want to leave, even if my body languished while my mind and her voice created this warm, soft illusion. It may have been insanity and it may have been a lie to want to remain here, to never see with my own eyes and my implants again. I did want to remain though, regressed and sealed away from the nightmare of the world outside the womb.

"Say the word," the mother's voice said.

"What?" I couldn't cry anymore. My faceless fetus body may have even lacked tear ducts for all I knew. The word was something I didn't know, and I tried to ask again. "What's the word?"

I pulled myself along the umbilical cord, gripping it as tightly as I would have held Mary if I only could have found my eyes, my body, my manhood again. Being reduced like this was a balance between humiliation and heaven. It was the former if I had to go back to the world, and the latter if I could hide here forever. The only problem was that I didn't know the word, and I feared I never would.

I awoke an hour later, and she charged me double because I had slept so long.

Joseph Hirsch's other titles

Veterans' Affairs

The Bastard's Grimoire

www.ingramcontent.com/pod-product-compliance
Lightning Source LLC
Chambersburg PA
CBHW010448100726
47904CB00008B/2529